Sinful Duty

by
Euryia Larsen

Description

Konstantin Baranov

As Pakhan of the Baranov Bratva, it is my duty to marry well and produce a strong heir. A marriage alliance with the Zima Family is a wise move but I've already refused to marry Patrina Zima. To avoid insulting them further and starting a war, I've agreed to marry her sister Gianna. If she's a copy of her sister, war be damned, I'll end her myself.

Gianna Zima

Being a woman in the mafia means your only worth is in the name of your family and in the heir you can produce. A good marriage is unusual. A happy marriage is rare. A marriage of love is unheard of. Can I find peace with the giant Russian man with a scowl that is fearsome?

Chapter 1

Konstantin

"Kostya, to be honest, I'm relieved you aren't marrying Patrina. She's a spoiled bitch that would only make you miserable. That being said, it also leaves me in a bind," Leonardo Zima, Don of the Zima Family said as we spoke over coffee.

"The same for me. Here I thought being Pakhan meant being in charge," I sighed before drinking my black coffee.

Leo nodded with a wry chuckle. "Tell that to my aunt and uncle."

"So how do we fix this? This alliance is good for both of us."

"Well, I have a suggestion but I'm not sure you'll be happy with it." I raised an eyebrow as I waited for him to explain. "Patrina has a younger sister, she was still underage when we first met but turned twenty-one just recently. Gianna is a sweet woman who is a gentle soul and despite being raised in this world has a kind heart."

"If she is anything like Patrina..." I didn't complete that thought but I didn't need to either. Leo knew what was at stake, no matter how much we respected each other.

"She's not. But I must warn you. Hazel has made it clear that if any harm comes to Gianna she will hunt you down herself."

I couldn't help the chuckle that escaped as I thought about Leo's very pregnant wife. She was a joy and Leo was a lucky man. "I'm serious, Kostya. Never make a pregnant Irish lass mad. Truly terrifying!"

Laughing, I couldn't help but ask, "And just what did you do to discover this?"

"I decline to answer as a matter of self-incrimination."

"Well, you are Italian so…"

"Har Har, asshole. Shall I arrange a meeting?"

"Da, yes. If she comes with a threat from Hazel, she has to be better than her sister."

"I'll make it happen." I watched as he typed a message into his phone. "Will her father have an issue?"

"He'd prefer you to choose Patrina but he won't be a problem." He sent another message and then asked, "Dinner tonight or tomorrow at my house?"

I looked at him in surprise. Technically we weren't officially allies yet so the invite to his house for dinner took me by surprise. "Tonight is preferable. I'd like to get this handled."

"Tonight it is. I won't take Hazel out unnecessarily right now and I trust you not to betray me in my house. Trust is necessary to make this alliance work." The serious look on his face assured me he was being honest and I wouldn't be attacked.

5

"Agreed. If all goes well, soon we'll not only be allies but family as well and family is everything."

Gianna

I stood patiently waiting for my father, Aldo Zima, to acknowledge me. He often called us into his office and made us wait for him. It was all about power to my father. My cousin Leonardo Zima was the Don of the Zima family but my father as his uncle tried to act as if he were the head of the family. I knew at some point Leo would have to deal with him.

I watched as he stood up and walked around his desk to stand in front of me, appraising me as if I were something he owned. "Tonight we are going to Leo's home where you will meet your fiance. You will fulfill your duty to this family and ensure that a strong alliance with the Russians is in place. You will report to me anything of interest that I can use, am I clear?"

"Yes, father. If I may ask, how do I ensure a strong alliance and spy on them at the same time?" I only asked an innocent question but that didn't stop him from immediately slapping me as punishment for questioning him.

"You will do as I say and do not disrespect me again. If Konstantin Baranov rejects you as he did your sister, you will regret it, am I clear?" His threatening voice caused me to tremble in fear. I was always afraid of earning my parents' wrath. How I will ever be a proper wife I do not know. Patrina was always the perfect one, unable to do any wrong, that was until she was rejected by Konstantin. Now she will be married off to someone much less powerful.

I was unsure how I would be able to measure up. I was everything Patrina was not. I was a shy, plain girl who would rather read or draw quietly in a corner. Nothing that a powerful Pakhan would want. Unfortunately, that didn't seem to matter. I would do what my family demanded. That was my only choice. "Yes, father," I answered him softly. My hand wanted to hold my throbbing cheek but I knew that would only anger my father more.

"Go and make yourself presentable. Be ready at five o'clock. Not a minute after."

"Yes, father," I mumbled as I quickly left his office. I ran to my room and immediately headed towards the shower. I was determined to not embarrass my family and earn their anger.

Chapter 2

Gianna

It was five minutes before five o'clock and I took one last look in the mirror. My makeup was quite a bit heavier than I normally wore to cover the dark bruise on my cheek. My dark hair was kept long and I wore a simple yet pretty pale blue dress. It was similar to one Father had liked previously so I hoped he had no complaints this time.

Grabbing my small clutch purse that held my phone and wallet, I quickly headed down the stairs and toward the front door. I was pleased to see that I arrived at the same time as Father. He took one look at me and nodded. I sighed in relief. He was pleased.

I waited quietly to see who else was coming. Finally, Momma appeared with Patrina. I was surprised to see my sister joining us. Her breakup with Konstantin was quite an embarrassment to the family. I had a feeling Leonardo wouldn't be happy to see her but I knew better than to say anything. I remained quiet as we got into the SUV and started the short trip to Leo's home.

"Father, will that Irish woman be there?" Patrina asked in disgust.

Father looked up at Patrina with a scowl. "Unfortunately, yes. If you embarrass me yet again I'll end you myself. Am I clear?"

Patrina rolled her eyes but replied, "Yes, Father." She turned to look at me, a mean smile on her face. "Let me know if you want any tips on Konstantin, dear sister. His appetite is deliciously dark."

Momma gasped loudly at Patrina's words. Father ignored us all. This was how it normally was. I just turned my head and looked out the window. In truth I was terrified. Before Leonardo took over as Don, we'd been in a war with the Russians. Konstantin Baranov was only spoken of in hushed voices. He was said to rule the Bratva with an iron fist and dispatch enemies in some of the most gruesome ways.

Before I knew it, we'd arrived at Leo's home. I was looking forward to seeing Hazel again. She was the sweetest person and I could have cared less that she was Irish. She'd proven her loyalty to our Don and that was all that mattered to me. Leo was completely in love with his wife and I loved watching the two of them together.

I exited the vehicle and waited for Father to lead us to the front door. Along the way, Momma fidgeted with my dress before sighing and muttering, "I guess that will have to do. It's too bad you aren't as pretty as your sister."

I briefly closed my eyes to the stinging pain of her words. Shoving it into the back corner of my mind, I kept my attention on not being an embarrassment. I watched as Leo opened the door and heard a happy squeal as Hazel burst forth and pulled me into a tight hug. I loved that Leo let her be herself and didn't expect her to act like a perfect robot with no emotions.

"Gianna!" She whispered into my ear, "Don't worry, I got your back girl. Kostya has been properly threatened by me."

Hazel was tiny like me and the idea that she threatened the Pakhan of the Baranov Bratva had me fighting a giggle that wanted to burst forth.

"I see your wife has still to learn respect, Leonardo," Father glared.

The smile on Leo's face turned into a dark scowl. "Control your tongue or else, Aldo," he warned.

Father didn't like that. He hated that he hadn't been named Don of the Zima family. He felt he deserved it. After all, the previous Don was his older brother. Instead, the role had gone to Leo as the direct heir. Father didn't respond to Leo's warning but instead asked, "Has the Russian arrived yet?"

As we entered the house and into the living room, I saw three of the largest scariest men I'd ever seen before. Father immediately stepped forward and held out his hand to the largest of the men who stood in the middle. "Konstantin."

"Aldo." As Konstantin greeted Father, his eyes stayed locked on me. I could feel the heat of a soft blush fill my cheeks.

"Kostya, you know my aunt and uncle and Patrina, but this is Gianna. Gianna, this is Konstantin Baranov, Pakhan of the Baranov Bratva," Leo introduced.

Konstantin immediately took my small hand in his and brought it to his lips, turning the pale blush on my cheeks to a flaming red. "You awe me with your beauty, zaika." My eyes stayed locked to his and realized that I could get lost looking into his storm-gray eyes.

"Let's give them a few minutes while we head into the dining room for a round of drinks," Leo suggested from far away and before long we were alone.

"Gianna, zaika, tell me about the things that make you smile."

I pulled my eyes away trying to collect my thoughts and remember how to use my words. I didn't know what it was about this man but I could already tell he was dangerous with that charm of his. "I-I love to read and draw or paint. S-silly things really."

"Not silly. Never that. Russians are cold by nature but we love and appreciate the beauty of the arts. I am no different. I look forward to seeing your art." He reached out to caress my cheek and without realizing I flinched from the pain his touch caused my bruised cheek.

Afraid he would be insulted, I tried to quickly apologize. "I-I'm…"

"Zaika, who hurt you? Who did this to you?" The anger in his eyes frightened me. His rage was almost tangible.

"It's nothing, I promise."

"Gianna, who disrespected you? As your intended, they insult me as well."

"It's nothing. I made Father angry. That is all. Please, this alliance is important. More important than a small mark on my cheek," I pleaded with him.

11

"For you, I will not respond. No one will ever touch you in this way again, zaika. I promise you this. Now, shall we join the others?" With a nod of my head, he took my hand and led me to the dining room. When he noticed that Patrina had made sure to sit next to Konstantin, he approached her and ordered, "Move."

Patrina gasped in horror at his order and looked indignantly at Father and then at Leo. When she realized no one was going to say anything, she stood up with a huff and moved to the seat next to Momma, putting her next to one of the men who was with Konstantin. The scowl on that man was frightening and I was glad it wasn't directed at me.

Chapter 3

Konstantin

Gianna was mine. It didn't matter that she was Patrina's sister. The moment my eyes met hers I knew that she was the woman meant for me. There was a softness, a kindness to her that reminded me of a soft bunny. She was my little bunny, my zaika.

The bruise on her cheek enraged me and Leo and I would be having a chat about it. If her family or any of the Zima's touched her again, they'd answer to me. Alliance be damned. It pissed me off to no end that Patrina dared to show her face to me. When I saw her in the chair that belonged to Gianna and only Gianna I almost pulled out my gun and shot her. I hated that woman. She was everything I despised.

After Patrina had moved and Gianna was seated, I was happy to see that Hazel was seated next to her. Hazel was as kind as she was beautiful and her love for my zaika made my heart smile.

I continued to hold Gianna's hand, unwilling to let it go. The sound of her father's voice grated on my nerves but I refused to allow him to know how much I disliked him. "As Gianna is more to your liking, when should we expect this alliance to be finalized?"

"Alliance? I thought this was a marriage to unite two families but yet still a marriage." I stated. "As for when, let's enjoy dinner, and then Don Zima and I can discuss business and any details. Agreed?"

Leo smirked as he replied, "Agreed. I loathe discussing business over a family meal."

"As do I. Zaika, have you met my younger brothers, Nikandr and Daniil?"

"I have not. It's lovely to meet you. May I ask, what does Zaika mean?"

"Little rabbit," Nikandr chuckled. "Brother, I never knew you to use such terms of endearment before. I do admit that Zaika is quite appropriate."

I watched as Gianna's cheeks turned an adorable pink.

"What was the pet name that you had for me, Kostya? Oh yes, suka. That was it. It sounds so tender and loving. Who knew how sweet a Russian could be." Patrina took a drink of her wine wearing a cruel smirk on her face.

Before I could give her a response, my ever-quiet brother, Daniil said, "Suka means bitch."

Both Patrina and her mother gasped whereas Hazel and Leo were fighting a losing battle not to laugh. I looked down at Gianna and while she had her hand over her mouth to give the appearance of horror, I noticed that in truth she wanted to laugh.

After dinner, my brothers and I followed Leo and Aldo into Leo's office. Once settled I stated, "Unless you have an injection, I would like to have this wedding business concluded tomorrow."

"I agree, the sooner the better," Leonardo nodded.

"Yet as her father, I do not agree. We haven't discussed how this alliance will serve our family. She is my daughter and I wouldn't feel right about putting her into the hands of our former enemies,"

Leo's eyes narrowed at his uncle. I could already see he would be a problem for him in the future. "Aldo, terms have already been agreed to,"

"Consider yourself lucky, Aldo. If I had my way I would have added your hands as part of the terms for touching what is mine." I glared darkly at Gianna's father before looking back at Leonardo.

"Aldo, have Gianna here by nine am. You may go." As the man stood to leave Leo added, "Touch her again and I will take offense."

By his breathing, I could tell the man was fuming but I also didn't care. Gianna would be away from them soon enough.

Gianna

My wedding day. I knew one day it would happen but I never thought it would happen so quickly. I didn't mind, I never wanted to be the center of attention so the faster it happened the faster it would be over. Even though I knew all eyes would be on me as the bride, the thought of Konstantin being with me calmed me.

After showering and getting dressed in jeans and a plain light blue shirt, I headed down the stairs to breakfast. Father was already sitting at the table and still fuming from the night before. "Good morning, Father."

"Did you pack your bags last night? Once this sham of a wedding is over you'll no longer be my problem."

I quietly sat down as a bowl of fruit was given to me. I sat quietly eating my breakfast, not wanting to make Father any madder. I looked up as he pushed an older-style flip phone to me. I quickly glanced up and looked at him.

"You will do as I say and take note of anything of interest. When I call, you will answer, am I clear? Fail me and I will take you out myself."

"Yes, Father." I would never want to spy on my husband. My loyalty was first and foremost to my husband and then to Leo. Once I left this house, Father's demands meant nothing to me. I wouldn't, I couldn't start my marriage off on a lie and mistrust. That wasn't who I was at my core.

Chapter 4

Gianna

The wedding had been simple but beautiful. Hazel had arranged for the perfect dress for me and when Konstantin saw me for the first time, the smile that filled his face made me so happy. It was the look every girl hoped to see on her groom's face. It was one I never thought I'd see. I expected to be married to some soldier as a reward for loyalty. I knew it would be a loveless marriage but one I prayed wouldn't be violent.

I still hoped it wouldn't turn violent once Konstantin realized how useless I was as the wife of a Pakhan. I didn't think Leo or Hazel would give me to a cruel man but this was a political marriage not a marriage of love, even though I hoped that was what it would turn into.

Konstantin had insisted on kissing me at the end of the ceremony and my lips still tingled from the kiss he'd given me. It was everything I'd hoped a first kiss would be like. Since then my new husband hadn't left my side. After one of his men had approached us and spoken to Konstantin in Russian I'd asked him, "Would you prefer me to learn Russian or should I allow you that privacy for business?"

His smile was gentle as he looked down at me. "Zaika, I leave that decision to you. I'm sure eventually you will learn some of my language from exposure to it, but I have no secrets. Ask me anything and I will tell you. If you prefer to not know then I am fine with that as well."

I smiled and nodded at his response. While I was getting ready for the wedding, Hazel had assured me that she liked Konstantin. His brothers made her nervous but she suspected that was due to their intensity.

We danced and mingled until it was finally time for us to leave. We were spending our first night in Leo's home which I will admit, made me nervous. Sensing my nervousness, Konstantin asked me, "You are aware of the tradition of first night, yes?" I nodded as I blushed hotly to his question. His finger caressed my cheek as he spoke softly to me. "I do not like this tradition but Leo said it was something your father insisted on as proof that you were accepted as my wife. I promise to make it as painless as possible."

"There will be pain. Hazel explained it all to me. I won't hate you for what you must do."

Konstantin leaned close as he softly kissed me before replying, "You honor me, my sweet Gianna. This may be a political marriage but it is my wish that this be a marriage with joy and love." I smiled at his words, praying that they were truths and not pretty lies. "When we return to my city where our home is at, there will be one bit of pain that I must insist upon. Every woman who is part of the Bratva receives a tattoo as a sign of their loyalty. It is also a matter of protection."

"What will it look like?"

"The women receive a flower laurel around their wrists. Baranov is written amongst the flowers. My name as your husband is written below Baranov in Cyrillic."

"That sounds beautiful. I would never have been allowed anything even remotely like a tattoo. Will it be terribly painful?"

"Ivan will numb the area first but it will be sore for a few days. I will never allow any to hurt you, Zaika."

"I know," I smiled. "This is to protect me as your wife so that enemies will think twice before attacking me."

Konstantin pulled me into his arms as he placed a kiss on my forehead and led us up to our room. I squealed and a nervous giggle escaped as suddenly he scooped me up into his arms and carried me the rest of the way. Konstantin chuckled as he held me close. Closing the door behind us he sat me on the edge of the bed. "That musical sound of joy is one I hope to hear often, sweet Gianna."

"Konstantin, there is something I must tell you before we do anything else. I don't want there to be any secrets or lies in our marriage." I watched as he bent down on his knee, giving me his full attention. Pulling out the phone from my clutch I handed it to him as I explained, "Father wants me to spy on you and your bratva. He hates that Leo is Don and he hates the idea of the alliance even more."

"I suspected that he would do this. I thank you for telling me, sweet zaika. That means everything to me." He kissed me softly before standing up and placing the phone on the nightstand along with his items. He returned to me and pulled me up. Turning me around he looked at the back of my dress. He sighed loudly as he saw all the buttons. "Why do they make wedding dresses so complicated to take off? Men are not patient creatures."

I couldn't stop the giggle that I escaped as I looked over my shoulder at him. "Anything you do to the buttons can be repaired later."

His eyes shot up to mine as a wicked smile filled his handsome face. My skin tingled as my core dampened. That man was so handsome and when he smiled that way at me, he was breathtaking.

Suddenly he ripped apart the back of my dress, buttons flying in all directions. At the sight of my bare back, Konstantin leaned close and kissed down my back from my shoulders. "All I want to do is love you in every way possible. I never want to be the cause of your pain."

I blinked at him, speechless. "You want to love me? But what if I'm a horrible wife?"

Konstantin turned me around to look at him, his giant hands holding my face as his thumbs caressed my cheeks. Leaning forward he kissed me ever so softly before whispering, "How could I not? You're my little beauty, my zaika. I refuse to believe that you are 'horrible' at anything you want to do."

I gasped as tears of joy filled my eyes. I captured his face in my hands. "My dangerous, sweet husband."

"Only with you Gianna," He moaned as he pulled me into his arms and his lips claimed mine in a passionate kiss. He tasted me as I released a soft sigh granting him entrance. He deepened the kiss as it turned possessive.

Breaking away from my lips, he leaned his forehead against mine and closed his eyes as he tried to maintain control. "I worry that I'm too big. Trust me to prepare your body to take me without too much pain." As I nodded, his arms tightened around me, holding me close. "You'll tell me if I hurt you."

It wasn't a request, it was an order in a dominant way that I found incredibly sexy. Gently raising my face so that I looked at him, he stated in a husky voice, which made me tingle all over, "I promise to love, honor, and be faithful to you and only to you." With his proclamation, he stood up with me in his arms, his lips planting kisses all over my face. I couldn't hold back the giggles as I held onto him tightly.

In this world, mistresses and affairs were commonplace. I truly hoped his words remained true. I didn't know if I could handle knowing that my husband was not my own. It would destroy my heart and soul.

He laid me gently on the bed and kissed me so passionately that I knew my panties were completely soaked. As I sighed into his kiss, my body relaxed into his, our bodies touching as much as possible. My new husband immediately took my cue and deepened the kiss, his hands caressing my bare skin.

He broke the kiss only to stand up and remove my dress from my body, freeing my breasts for him to gaze upon. Under my wedding dress, I wore a white lace thong and a lacy soft pink garter on my thigh. My shoes had disappeared as he'd pulled the dress off.

He stood looking at me as my cheeks pinkened in shyness. "Do you have any idea how incredibly beautiful you are, my wife? I'm doing everything in my power to maintain control until your body is ready for me, but looking upon your beauty makes it nearly impossible."

He immediately bent down onto his knees and pulled me to the edge of the bed, placing my legs over his shoulders.

I was a virgin but that didn't mean I didn't know what happened in the bedroom. I enjoyed reading romances of all kinds. I wonder what he would say when he saw the boxes of books I was bringing. I just couldn't leave them behind.

He started to kiss one leg at the ankle and the closer he got, the wetter I became. Just as I thought he would taste me, he turned his attention to my other leg, pulling a loud moan from me. "Patience my zaika. Put your trust in your husband. I will not deny your pleasure tonight."

I gasped and moaned his name as I felt a hot molten-like sensation move down my body to my core. The wetness between my legs soaked through the small bit of lace covering my core. Scraping my nails over his scalp while I held he tasted and teased my body. His soft groan of pleasure caused my toes to curl in pleasure.

Konstantin rubbed his nose along the lace and moaned, "You are perfect my little bunny. This is the nectar of the gods that I feel blessed to enjoy." His poetic words wrapped around me and increased my desire for him to levels I think were possible. Suddenly he ripped the thong from my body and tossed it behind him to join where he'd also tossed the garter at some point.

I looked into his eyes as I lay bare before him. I fought against the desire to hide my body from him. Slowly, his fingers delicately explored every curve of my body. His fingers left a trail of heat as he moved down until he found my center. He dipped into my wetness before returning his attention to my bud. He started to pleasure me with his roughened fingers, smiling as he heard my gasp in response, eyes closing from the intense pleasure.

I opened myself to his touch. I felt as if I were drowning in it, but I didn't want to be saved. I just wanted him to keep touching me. I opened my eyes suddenly as I felt Konstantin move away from me. Then I realized that he wasn't. Instead, he replaced his fingers with his mouth,

"Konstantin!" I cried out before moaning loudly, "Oh!" I thrust my hips forward, wanting him to devour me, to continue to pleasure me. Ever higher, I climbed until I felt I would shatter from the intense pleasure. When his tongue joined his fingers, I completely shattered, crying out his name and shaking from the intense orgasm crashing through my body.

Chapter 5

Gianna

My husband moved back up as I slowly descended from the intenseness of the orgasm, kissing me tenderly as he held me close. A few minutes passed before I opened my eyes and looked at him wearing a smirk. I returned his wicked smile with one of my own as I reached down and massaged his cock through his pants. "You're still dressed," I whispered as I moved my fingers along the waistband of his pants.

I watched as he quickly stood and removed the clothing from his body. The man was all hard muscle and inked skin. I could just make out the scars that littered his body. The tattoos masked them so that one only saw hardened perfection.

As I looked at him standing there exposed to me, he smirked and I knew he enjoyed my eyes on him. Before long he climbed onto the bed and kissed me as if he wished to devour me. I let my fingers explore the hard ridges of his body before they reached his rather large cock. It was soft, so silky soft, yet with a hardness that rivaled stone.

Konstantin let me push him onto his back, watching to see what I was going to do. I crawled over and claimed his lips as mine. I kissed him while my fingers continued to explore his body. As I broke away from his lips, my eyes never left his as I crawled down his body. I placed kisses along the firm muscles of his abdomen.

Once I reached his perfect cock, I ran my tongue along his length as if it were an ice cream cone. I read this in nearly every book I'd read and had always wondered if it was true that men enjoyed a woman's mouth on them. By my husband's reaction, I knew it was.

His eyes rolled back into his head as I continued to explore his length with my mouth and fingers. The more I licked and sucked on him, the harder he became. There was more than I could fit into my mouth and down the back of my throat. What I couldn't take, I wrapped my hands around and gripped him tightly.

"Zaika," he groaned loudly as he gently but firmly held my head to him.

Before long, he was so close to the edge that he quickly grabbed me and rolled me under him. At my surprised look, he said, "I don't want to finish in your mouth for our first time, little bunny. I want you to come on my dick as I fill this beautiful pussy with every bit of my cum."

Konstantin kissed me, owning my mouth, as his hands left a trail of molten heat on my body. Feeling his cock rubbing at my slit, I spread my legs wide and opened to him fully, inviting him in as I whispered to him, "I am yours."

Closing his eyes at the pleasure my words brought to him, he slowly started to enter me, inch by stretching inch. He was so much bigger than my petite size, yet, despite our differences, we fit together perfectly. The burning sensation was a type of pain I could embrace and love. As he moved in and out of me gently to allow me to get used to his size, I moaned in pleasure at the sensations each of his movements brought to me.

When he reached the last remaining barrier between us, he said against my lips, "I'm sorry for the pain, Gianna. Forgive me." With a hard thrust, he tore through my virginity and filled me completely.

A scream tore out of me and I held onto him desperately. Hiding my face in his neck as tears escaped. He held me tightly to him and didn't move as the pain slowly eased. "I'm so sorry, my sweet girl. Never again will I hurt you. Please forgive me. I'm so sorry."

I held onto him, soaking up his love until finally, I needed him to move. I wanted him to move. I pulled back and kissed Konstantin's lips. "There is nothing to forgive, husband. Now I am yours and will only ever be yours."

For several long moments, he looked into my eyes. A soft smile formed before he captured my lips in a passionate kiss and slowly moved in and out of my body. I let instinct take control of my body's movement as I started to meet him stroke for stroke.

I felt a warm, tingling sensation building up along the base of my spine. The look in his eyes took my breath away. He was pouring his love into me. That one thought pushed me over the edge. A scream echoed through the house as my orgasm couldn't be held back. With one final powerful thrust, Konstantin joined me, filling me with his release.

We lay there for several minutes, breathing hard, entwined in each other's arms. My husband smiled as he hugged me closer to his body. A few minutes later he broke away from me, getting out of bed. He turned around and grabbing my ankle pulled me to the edge of the bed before scooping me up in his arms as I yelped. A giggle escaped as I wrapped my arms around his neck. I loved when he picked me up, it made me feel treasured by him. He walked us into the bathroom as he explained, "I thought we could soak our sore muscles in the bath."

I smiled as I looked at the large tub, which was not only large enough for him, but it was large enough for two of him. With a smile, I told him, "That's a wonderful idea."

Once the bath was filled with warm water, Konstantin climbed into the tub before he lifted me into the water with him. He placed a tender kiss on my shoulder before he sat down in the deep tub, motioning for me to join him. Sitting down in the water, I positioned myself between his legs and leaned back onto his chest, making sure to nestle gently between us.

He wrapped his arms around me and his fingers gently drifted along the underside of my breasts. "Your skin is softer than silk," he murmured as he kissed and tasted the skin along my shoulder.

"Mmmm..." was all I could say in that exquisite moment. The more he touched and tasted my warm skin, the more I enjoyed it. Feeling his cock hardening once again, I turned my head to capture his lips in a bruising kiss.

"You make me insatiable, my zaika."

I smiled seductively at him as I completely turned my body around until I was facing him. Raising on my knees, I positioned myself over him as I caressed him up and down with my hand. Claiming his lips again, I lowered myself onto him, causing him to groan from the pleasure. Up and down, I moved my body as his hands pinched and teased my breasts as our lips continued our passionate kiss.

Before long, he grabbed hold of my hips and began meeting me, thrust for thrust. Each movement brought us ever closer to the edge until suddenly we found our release together. I continued riding him, drawing out our pleasure until finally, I collapsed onto his chest. It was short, fast, and perfect.

"You, my beautiful Gianna, are amazing," Konstantin murmured into my hair.

I smiled softly as I lay in his arms. After several long minutes, I asked, "Why did Leo call you Kostya yesterday?"

"Many Russian names have a shortened form that friends and family may use. Kostya is the shortened version of Konstantin. It's more playful and relaxed in comparison. You may use either to your heart's desire, my sweet wife."

"Kostya. Konstantin. Kostya. I like it. When I was little, Leo would call me little Gia. I always loved it. To me, it was an expression of fondness and love."

"Gia is very sweet but you will always be my little bunny, my zaika."

Chapter 6

Konstantin

Taking the sheets to show Gianna's virginal blood was something I refused to subject Gianna to. I could tell Leo disliked it even more than I did and I appreciated it when he refused to let the men hang it like some sort of trophy. The sooner we left this place and returned to our territory the better I would feel.

My men had already loaded all of my zaika's items into our vehicles, making sure to let me know about the boxes of books and art supplies. I already had plans to create a library and art room for her. Gianna deserved the best of everything and I wanted to do all in my power to fill her days with joy.

I left the phone with Leo to handle it as he wanted and as the weeks that followed passed by, I heard how Leo was dismantling Aldo's power piece by piece until everything he had left was in a warehouse in my territory. That led to my current phone conversation with the Don of the Zima family. "The man is your uncle but his warehouse is in my territory."

"Destroy it, take it, I leave it up to you. I just want it gone. The final step will be a bullet. No one betrays me or the Zima Family."

I looked over to my brother, Daniil, and nodded. "You just made Daniil smile. He likes to make things go boom, probably a little too much."

"At least he doesn't dissect a man's testicles just because he can. I swear there is something seriously wrong with Dante." Dante Zima was known as the executioner of the Zima family. His talent for information extraction was legendary.

"At least he works for you. How is his wife?"

"She's doing well. Ready to have that baby. I can't wait to see how big bad Dante deals with dirty diapers." I laughed at the image. "How is Gianna settling in there?"

"Well. She fainted during the tattooing but was happy once it was over. I'm turning one of the rooms into a library for her books. When I gave her the credit card I expected her to go shopping like every other woman I knew. Instead, she just purchased more books."

Leo chuckled before saying, "That sounds like Gia. Is she still painting? She is so talented. Hazel wants to hang one of her pieces in the house. She's been complaining that the walls are too white and too empty. She managed to get a group of our deadliest men and had them paint the nursery and build all the furniture."

Talking with Leo was always enjoyable. We could relate with the both of us being married to tiny dynamos. "We turned the sunroom into her art studio because it gets the best light. She's awaiting multiple boxes of art supplies before she can paint. Apparently, her parents felt her art was something a wife didn't need to worry about so they rarely provided her with supplies."

"I was aware. I made sure to send her supplies every so often. It pleases me that she's able to bloom and be happy there.

She deserves it. Well, I need to hunt down my wife before dinner. Call me if anything happens regarding Aldo."

"We'll take care of the warehouse. Be safe Don Zima."

"Be safe Baranov Pakhan."

As I hung up the phone Gianna knocked softly before entering my office. "Hello, my beautiful bunny. What are you up to?"

"I just finished organizing the bookshelves but I need one moved and I can't find anyone to help me."

I stood up and immediately pulled her into my arms. Placing a kiss on the top of her head I said, "Come my zaika. Show me how I can help."

"Oh but aren't you busy?"

"Later I have to head out for a couple of hours but right now I am yours to command, my queen. How can your humble servant serve you?" Her responding giggle was everything I needed to hear. How I loved this woman.

Chapter 7

Gianna

I just finished showering when my phone rang somewhere. I tensed. No one called me, ever. I ran out of the bathroom, rushed to the living room, and looked for my phone. Just as I found it under the throw pillow on the couch, it stopped ringing so I checked the missed calls and saw Patrina's number.

Something must have happened if she was calling me. I returned the call as I walked back into the bedroom to put some clothes on. "Gianna," she says the moment the call connects. "I need you to come here right away. Hurry. It's Momma."

The line went dead, and a feeling of dread collected in my stomach. What happened to Momma? Why didn't Patrina tell me anything more? I tried calling her again, but she didn't answer, so I threw on the first clothes I found. I tried to call Kostya but it simply rang.

So I took my phone and purse and ran out of the apartment.

It never dawned on me that the guards weren't guarding the door. It should have. When I got to the street, I started looking around for a taxi, too distracted by all the possibilities of what could have happened to Momma to notice the car that was stopped right in front of me. "Gianna!" I hear my father's voice coming from the car. "Let's go." He opened the passenger's door, and without thinking it over, I got inside the car.

The sound of doors locking makes my head snap up to glare at my father, who is regarding me with malice in his eyes.

"Gianna," he sneered and backhanded me with such force that I blacked out.

Konstantin

I was just parking my car when my phone pinged with an incoming message. Thinking it must be Gianna, I opened the message and my blood turned ice cold. It was an image of Gianna sitting in a metal chair, hands tied behind her back. She was looking up, probably at the person who took the photo, her face a mask of anger and fear.

A big red bruise covered most of her cheek, her lip was split, and a thin line of blood trailed down from the corner of her mouth. The phone in my hand rang, showing Aldo Zima's number. "I'm going to kill you, Aldo," I growled the moment I took the call. "I'll make sure it's slow and painful."

"I'll send you the address. You come alone or I'm going to hurt her." The message with an address somewhere in the suburbs arrived after he cut the call.

I put the car into reverse and floored the gas pedal. I immediately called my brother and ordered, "Meet me at the address I'm sending. Aldo has taken Gianna." I hung up as fast as I called and quickly sent the address. Aldo wanted me to come alone but I was stupid. My brother would bring our best men and surround the place as I dealt with Aldo. Even if he killed me, he would never escape alive.

It took me far too long to reach the run-down house on the outskirts of town. It was a crumbling structure surrounded by overgrown grass and weeds. Two cars are parked off to the side. The door hung open barely hanging on its hinges. Two men stood on either side of the door, and another beside one of the cars.

I sent a quick message to Nikandr, providing him with intel and instructing him to get here right away. I took my gun from under my seat and headed toward the house. It was time to get my wife back.

Gianna

I watched my father as he leaned back on the boxes across from me, holding a gun in his hand. He wouldn't kill me, I knew that much. Aldo might be a bastard, but he wouldn't kill his daughter, would he? It suddenly hit me that I wasn't sure what he might do.

I had no idea what was going on, but it was evident that something happened. Something big because I had never seen my father in this state. The suit he wore was in shambles. His carefully slicked-back hair was in disarray, and even though his posture was relaxed, the hand on his knee was trembling slightly as his thumb tapped his leg in a fast pattern.

I knew his tells. He was angry, but based on the look in his eyes, he was also scared. Not good. "I had everything planned. It was perfect," he said, looking at the wall behind me. "Every single detail. It was brilliant! Pull the Bratva into a war, and then take over everything. A wedding shooter was supposed to take out Leonardo as well as Konstantin. He ran scared of the Russians. Stupid idiot."

I just stared at him in shock. Our whole family was at that wedding! They could have killed us. Did he even care?

"I was so confident that everything would go as planned until your husband blew up my warehouse last night. A hundred million. Gone. Leonardo probably knows already. I'm fucked." He looks down at me, and a crazy smile spreads across his face. "But I'm not going down alone. I'm going to kill that son of a bitch husband of yours if that's the last thing I do."

The sound of a car approaching reached my ears, and my blood ran ice cold. No. Please God, no. I tugged harder on the restraints I'd been trying to untie for the past thirty minutes. My right wrist was already raw. I just needed to loosen the rope a little bit more and I'll be able to pull out my hand. A shot rings out in front of the house. Two more follow in quick succession.

"That bastard." My father stood up and walked towards me. I leaned back in the chair to hide my hands from his view. He stopped on my right and raised his gun to my temple just as Konstantin burst in through the door. Our gazes collided, and for a moment, all I could do was watch him frozen there, seemingly in perfect control on the outside. His eyes focused on the gun at my temple. "Did you kill my men?" my father sneered.

"Yes. Let Gianna go. This is between the two of us, Aldo."

"I don't think so. I think I'd prefer to have her watch. It's all her fault anyway. Isn't it, Gianna?" He looked down at me with such hatred that my breath caught in my lungs. "You just couldn't do as I said. I was so thrilled when I heard you would be marrying the Pakhan himself. Oh, the plans I had. You know, I wonder . . . do you know why they call him Konstantin the Monster?"

"Aldo, don't," Kostya said, his eyes never leaving me or the gun at my temple.

"Oh, you didn't tell her?" My father laughed, grabbed my chin with two fingers, and turned my head so I was forced to look at Kostya. "Look at your husband, Gia."

Mikhail was staring at me, his body tense and his jaw tight, but he didn't say anything. I already knew how powerful he was. In this world, you never came into such power without spilling blood.

"He tortured people, Gianna. He killed your brother and your cousins. He tortured them to make them talk. Look at him well and see the real man you sold your family out for."

I looked at Kostya, willing him to say something. He doesn't. Instead, he mouthed without a sound, "I love you, I'm sorry."

I closed my eyes and took a deep breath. The world we lived in was a fucked-up thing. I always knew that, and I would be only deceiving myself by believing that Kostya could be anything other than another product of that criminal world. Each item of clothing I owned and every meal I had ever eaten had been paid for with blood money.

Did I condone violence? No. Could I torture a person to get the information I needed? Probably not. I opened my eyes and looked right into those beautiful eyes of his. Would I love Kostya any less because of what he did? No. A fucked-up world created fucked-up people. It was war, there will always be death in a war.

I was probably more fucked up than most because I accepted my reality for what it was. "I love you," I mouthed the words to Konstantin and watched him go still as he focused on my lips.

"My God, you're in love with him," my father stated in awe and then burst out laughing. "But no worries, we'll find you another monster to marry easily enough." He turned to Kostya. "Take out the magazine and drop the gun."

I watched, horrified as Kostya released the gun magazine and then threw it along with the gun on the floor in front of him. No, no, no, I couldn't lose him, I couldn't.

"There are handcuffs on the radiator in the corner." My father nodded towards the other side of the room, still pressing the gun to my head. "Cuff yourself."

Panic rose in my stomach as I watched my husband walk toward the radiator, put one side of the handcuff on his right wrist and closed the other around the pipe. My father was going to kill him.

"Aldo, please. Let Gianna go. You can do whatever you want with me, but let your daughter go."

"I don't know . . ." He lowered the gun and took a few steps toward Kostya. "I think I should let her watch me kill you. Maybe it will make her more obedient."

Ignoring the searing pain, I pulled on my restraints with all my might, rotating my hand left and right. At the same moment when I felt my hand slip free, a gunshot pierced the air. My head snapped up and I watched in horror as blood started pooling from the wound in Kostya's shoulder.

"You didn't think I'd let you off easy, did you? I have several more bullets here, and I'll make sure only the last one is fatal." Father took another step toward Kostya and cocked his head to the side. "What should I pick next? A leg maybe? Or the other shoulder? You could give me guidelines, it's your specialty."

I sprung to my feet and ran for Kostya's gun on the floor.

"Gianna!" my father yelled. "What the fuck do you think you're doing? Leave that thing alone. You'll hurt yourself, you idiot!"

"Get out and run!" Kostya shouted at the same time. "Fucking now, Gianna!"

I ignored them both. I wasn't running, and I was certainly going to hurt someone. And that someone wouldn't be me. I looked up at my father, who was standing in front of Kostya, and took the gun in one hand, inserted the magazine, and cocked the gun. It took me no more than a few seconds. I had practiced many times with my guards as a child.

The look in my father's eyes as he watched me stand up and aim the gun at him was priceless. For a few moments, the two of us just stood there looking at each other, my gun pointed at my father's chest as he regarded me. "You don't have the guts, Gianna." He smiled and started turning toward Kostya.

No, I didn't have the guts to kill my father. I took a deep breath, aimed at his thigh, and pulled the trigger. Aldo Zima screamed, and his gun fell from his hand. He crumpled to the floor, clutching his bloody thigh.

I took a couple of steps until I was standing right in front of him. "That's for me," I rasped, then I aimed again, this time at his shoulder, and fired. His body jerked and he fell backward onto the floor. "That's for . . . my husband."

Ignoring my father's weeping, I kicked his gun towards the other side of the room. "Gianna, give me the gun, zaika." I looked up at Kostya and his outstretched arm, walked to him, and put the gun in his free hand.

Konstantin

"Gianna, look at me, zaika." She raised her eyes to mine, and I saw the tears in her eyes. "Can I kill him, baby?"

I looked over at Aldo who was panting on the floor. If Gianna wasn't here, he would already be dead, but I wouldn't kill him in front of her unless she wanted me to. She nodded her head, then pulled off her T-shirt and squeezed it into a bundle.

39

Standing there in only her bra and jeans, she pressed her shirt to my bleeding shoulder.

My hand was still cuffed to the radiator pipe, and my shoulder was screaming in pain, but there was no way I'd risk her going near that bastard to find the key. Instead, I wrapped my free arm around her and held her to my chest, making sure that the gun in my hand didn't touch her skin.

The door banged into the wall and Nikandr and Daniil rushed in, guns drawn, looking around.

"Eyes to the floor," I barked. No one was seeing my wife half naked except for me, special circumstances be damned. "The key to the cuffs." I motioned with my head toward Aldo. "Call Leo to have someone pick him up and deliver his body back to them."

At my words, Daniil shot Aldo between the eyes before bending down to search for the keys. Once he found them, he tossed them to Nikandr to unlock the cuffs for me. "We need to get you looked at, brother," he said as he looked at my shoulder.

"Let's go home. Doc can meet us there." I placed a finger under Gianna's chin and raised her head. "Are you okay, zaika?"

She took my hand and placed it on the shirt she'd been pressing into my shoulder, cupped my face with her hands, and kissed me. "No. But I will be." She says and kisses me again.

"We need to set up some rules. When I tell you to run, you run, Gianna. Is that clear?"

"And leave you to be killed?"

"Yes." Aldo could have killed her. I didn't think he'd do that, but I would never risk her life, even if there was a one percent possibility that she would end up hurt.

"I can't promise you that. I'm sorry."

"Gianna, zaika, if you don't promise me, I'm going to lock you in that room and put two men at the door. Please don't test me on this."

"Okay."

"Okay, what? Okay, you promise you'll do as I say?"

She smirked a little, put her arms around my waist, and placed her head on my chest.

Epilogue

Gianna

The weeks following the death of my father were chaotic. I was happy that the alliance held strong despite the actions of one man determined to ruin everything in search of power. I refused to attend Father's funeral with the support of Leo. I was loyal to the Baranov Bratva but the Zima Family was still in my heart.

As I looked out the large window, I felt strong arms wrap around me. I smiled as Kostya planted kisses on the cheek and neck. What has you thinking so hard, Zaika?"

"Everything and nothing. I was marveling at how much my life has changed since I first met you. It feels like I found the missing half of me and that I've always loved you. I love you so much that it sometimes terrifies me. Please don't ever break my heart, Kostya."

"Never. You are everything to me. You're my heart, my soul, my peace." He turned me around in his arms and captured my lips. Picking me up, he carried me to our bedroom, never breaking our kiss.

"Love me always, Konstantin." I spoke the words at the same time that I reached between us and gripped his cock through the material of his jeans. A blaze of intense passion ignited between us, stronger than ever before.

He kissed me, his hands running over my back, my ass. They grazed the soft, outer rounds of my breasts. I wrapped one of my arms around his back as I tightened my grip on his cock. He nuzzled my cheek with his nose, "This is us, Gianna. I love you, my fierce little bunny."

My heart leaped and every muscle in my body melted at his words. His large, strong hands gripped my hips, and he made a sound that was part growl, part need. Wrapping my arms tightly around his neck, I pulled him down onto the bed with me. I opened my legs to allow his erection to press against my center.

Lifting my hips, he slid his hard rod into me, rocking the steeliness over my clit. Gasping, I gripped his head, pressing my lips to his. His kiss was devouring, his movements hypnotizing as I undulated my hips in motion with his. He felt so good. I hadn't even stripped off one article of clothing yet, and I was already so close.

I moaned, and his hand found its way between us, his thumb covering my clit through the material of my jeans. It was pressing then brushing over that sensitive spot slowly, then faster, teasing in slow circles.

When I released the button on my jeans, his fingers took over, pulling down my zipper before slipping inside my underwear. His fingers massaged my clit before pinching it. My orgasm hit hard and fast. "Kostya," I moaned. Colors exploded behind my eyelids as my orgasm drenched his hands as he continued his torturous caresses.

"That's it, baby. Let go. I have you and I'll never let you go," this gorgeous man murmured into my ear as the wave crashed over me. When I could open my eyes again, Kostya smiled at me as he pushed my hair out of my face. He gripped my shirt, pulling it over my head and doing the same with his own. I watched him with hooded eyes. He pulled my jeans off but left me in my underwear.

As he stood in front of me, he removed his pants. I ogled the large tent in his boxer briefs. I couldn't help but lick my lips at the thought of the pleasure he would give me with it. "Come here," he said, pulling me to him for another hot kiss. When he came up for air, his hands quickly removed my bra, throwing it over his shoulder as his eyes never left my breasts. Taking a nipple into his mouth, I gasped at the pleasurable sensations he created while sucking, nipping, and pinching my nipples. "Your skin tastes sweet like the finest fruit."

Before I had a chance to reply, he was moving down my body, licking and nipping my skin as he removed the last of our clothing. The sensations turned me on so much that I felt like I was about to combust. His hands pulled down my soaked panties as he dragged a finger between my folds. "Kostya," I moaned as my back arched, and my hands dug into the blankets on our bed.

Kostya made a sound low in his throat as he gripped my waist, his mouth devouring mine. He was big and tall and I felt so safe surrounded by him, my mind, and my body fully encompassed by this man. Raising my hips higher, he guided the tip of himself to my entrance. The head pressed its way in stretching me in the best way possible.

He paused briefly until my hips began to move on their own, my need overcoming everything else. As if he sensed that desperation, he plunged the entire length of his hardness deep inside me until he was seated as far as he could go.

I cried out as the pleasure took over everything. Words, thoughts, everything was gone, leaving only pleasure. The only thing left was this man and his body as it became one with me. More. I wanted… "More."

Kostya drew back until he nearly left my body. He paused just long enough to have my pussy muscles clenching in anticipation before he impaled me. I moaned loudly as he did it again, going as deep as possible each time.

My legs tightened around his hips, my arms around his neck. I held him as close to me as possible as I moaned into his ear, "I want everything, all of you."

His hands gripped me tighter, the sound of our skin slapping together making me toss back my head. Growling my name, he pistoned into me. Our bodies moved together so fast the headboard banged against the wall.

A tingling began in my pussy, growing and spreading out until my whole body was vibrating with it. My inner muscles tightened around his even harder cock. My name was a chant on his lips as the feeling swept me higher, and his thrusts moved my body across the bed.

The sound he made told me he was close. With that single thought, my orgasm slammed into me pulling every muscle taut as he buried himself deep in my body, holding me tight and still as he pulsed inside me. My eyes rolled up in my head, my back bent as my body arched even closer to my Konstantin. My body trembled and vibrated as he pumped into me, emptying himself as one swell after another crashed through me.

Pulling me against his chest, he placed a tender kiss on my forehead as he held me in his arms. I smiled as I lay in his arms, moving with the rise and fall of his chest matching mine. "I love you, Gianna. I will always love you.

I smiled up at this man, my husband, my everything. Whatever the future held for us, I knew I could handle it with him by my side. "I love you, my handsome Russian bear." He chuckled as he nuzzled my neck, making me giggle.

As long as we had each other, we had everything.

The End

About the Author

Euryia Larsen grew up thinking that what she was being told about the world was only part of the story. She loves myths both historical and modern and often sees the the possibility in 'what if'. A good romance with strong 'alpha' heroes and even stronger heroines that can be a partner for them are her favorite kinds of books. If the heroines are just a tad crazy, even better.

Euryia is a stay at home mom of two beautiful daughters, three crazy cats, three crazier dogs and a husband to round out the bunch. She deals with her fair share of issues while dealing with Fibromyalgia and other complications and as a result, she's finds an escape in books where there is always a happily ever after. She's always been creative and has written for herself as an audience for longer than she can remember.

I'd love to hear your thoughts on this or myths or books in general or even just a hello.

Check me out at
http://www.EuryiaLarsen.com
or feel free to email me at
EuryiaLarsenAuthor@gmail.com

Other Books by Euryia Larsen

Broken Butterfly Dreams

Standalone Novellas:

The Mobster's Violet

Clover's Luck

Touch of Gluttony

Halloween Darkness

Another Notch On Her Toolbelt

Sealed With A Kiss

Fate's Surprise

Midnight Rose

His Curvy Housemaid

Hello, Goodbye

The Dark Side (Dragon Skulls MC):

Saint

Beautiful Smile

Twisted Savior

Belladonna Club:

To Trap A Kiss

His Peridot

Zima Family:

Devil's Desire

Cursed Angel

Baranov Bratva:

Sinful Duty

Sweet Child of Mine

Menage Series:

Masked Surprise

Sweet Cherry Pie

Home on the Ranch

Perfect Storm

Curveball

Lonesome Shadows

Cursed Guardians

Love is Love Boxsets:

Menage A Trois

Affaire de Coeur

Not the Good Guy (Kazon Brothers)

with Kyra Nyx:

Kazon Brothers Box Set

The Dark

The Beast

The Villain

Saga of The Realms:

Power of Love – Prequel Novella (Paperback)

Power of Love – Prequel Novella (Free Ebook)

Bonded By Destiny

War of Giants

Printed in Great Britain
by Amazon

COMPASSIONATE LEADERSHIP

Creating Places of Belonging

CHRIS WHITEHEAD

First published in 2019 by Solopreneur Publishing, West Yorkshire U.K., an imprint of Oodlebooks.

www.oodlebooks.com

The Solopreneur Publishing Company Ltd focuses on the needs of each author client. This book has been published through their 'Solopreneur Self-Publishing (SSP)' brand that enables authors to have complete control over their finished book whilst utilising the expert advice and services usually reserved for traditionally published print, in order to produce an attractive, engaging, quality product. Please note, however, that final editorial decisions and approval rests with the author.

ISBN 978-1-9164415-4-5

Printed in the U.K.

Developmental edit by Richard Bateman

DEDICATION

To those managers I've met whose practice has been deeply human and effective in consequence. John Gregory, George Marsden, Anthony Rabin, Mike Archbold, Dave Donaldson, Jane Whitfield, Mike Peasland and Ed and Tom Westgate. With gratitude.

TABLE OF CONTENTS

Dedication

Table of Contents

Foreword

Introduction 1

Part 1: Understanding the Human Mind **11**

The Brain 11

The Mind and Body 19

Human Agency 25

Attachment 29

Transference 35

Projection 39

Defence Mechanisms 43

Personality Disorders 49

Unfinished Business and Emotional Bandwidth 57

Motivational Needs and Addiction 61

Transactional Analysis 67

Theories of Human Development 73

Systemic Thinking 79

Bridge into Part 2 83

Part 2: Compassion for One Another **89**

Treating One Another as Individuals 89

Authenticity and Vulnerability 95

Trust 99

Carl Rogers 107

PACE 113

Handling Strong Emotions in Others 119

Managing Upwards 123

Managing Individual Performance 129

The Leader as Coach 135

Part 3: Compassion for Teams **143**

People, Product, and Profit 143

Creating a Compassionate Culture 147

Leading Organisational Change 157

Emotional Intelligence in Teams 165

Team Development 171

How to Recruit Like the Duke 179

Appreciative Inquiry 183

Flexible Working 187

The Life-Giving Workforce Design Model 191

Part 4: Compassion for Yourself **199**

Personal Resilience 199

Dealing with Sociopaths 205

Finding Your Vocation 211

Personal Development 217

Creating Personal Meaning 227

Your Locus of Control 132

Conclusion 235

Food for Thought 239

References 241

Index 257

Table of Figures 261

About the Author 263

FOREWORD

I was driving home from the office one Friday evening when my phone rang - it was my colleague Nick. "Ade, you know I was talking to you about Chris Whitehead and his book Compassionate Leadership, he wondered if you would write the foreword." To say I was shocked is an understatement – I haven't written many book forewords. I asked somewhat hesitantly "Why me?" "Well, the book reflects your style of management, maybe the two of you should get together and discuss."

Chris and I met up at the Bridge Inn, Holmfirth. We ordered coffee and then started to talk. We hit it off straight away – it was clear there was a connection, and I was interested to know more about Chris, his book, the ideas behind it and his motivation to write it.

Over the years I have learned that books are very very personal. There is a lot that goes on in the mind and depending upon where you are in your life; the same book can take on different meanings at different times.

Chris' style of writing took me right back to the beginning of my working life. It was 1989; I was studying graphic design; my parents had separated. Marker pens were expensive, so I took a job as a banqueting wine waiter at the Hilton Hotel in Kensington. We had a manager, Karen –until now I had not reflected on her style of leadership, but Chris's book prompted me to.

She was open; she listened to us, she made our case to 'upper management', she held values which were centred around teamwork and putting the customer first, she allowed us to have fun (within reasonable boundaries!). We often worked until

3-4am, weekdays and weekends – we were knackered most of the time, but I found a corner in the college library next to the radiator and slept there during lunch times. It was hard graft, but we loved it, and at the end of the evening, she would buy us all a beer.

There was a great sense of camaraderie and customers would comment on what great service they received. We trusted her, and she trusted us, treating us as equals, one team - she allowed us to be ourselves. She treated us with respect, and we reciprocated.

In the summer of 1990, Karen was poorly. It was the wedding season. We turned up to work to report to a stand-in-manager, and everything changed. We were all told what to do, and how to do it and how we were not doing it right (or good enough).

Fortunately, Karen recovered and returned to work four weeks later, and we were all back to normal (phew!). The contrast was quite incredible. Had Karen not returned, there is no doubt we would have found other jobs. Instead, we stayed together as a team until 1991, when I finished college and started my own design agency.

Who should read Chris's book? My answer to that question is me, the Adrian Brown of 1996, five years into running an agency, believing that managing people is about telling them what to do, imagining he doesn't have the time to read management books and in any event unconvinced that books will enlighten him and accelerate his career.

In the 25 years that followed, I rethought those beliefs, went on to read over 50 books, and worked with nearly 100 companies and their senior managers. I orchestrated some great successes and also some major balls-ups, and I reflected deeply in order to re-align my thinking on what it means to lead.

This equipped me for running the medical device business my dad set up in 2003. It's a company that my team and I have reimagined, putting patient outcomes and clinician training at its core. The business now draws on all my hard-won people skills – to lead 25 brilliantly talented people, manage rapid growth and recruit new staff that have a passion for med tech.

I am forever conscious of my day-to-day leadership role: to help, to support and to guide, whilst ensuring an environment that is safe, open, engaging, exciting, supportive and fulfilling. I think Andy Cope nails it when he uses the term 'Pop-Up Leadership' – I like that. There are however days (or even weeks) that are tough, sometimes we get it right and sometimes we don't. The important thing is to reflect, learn, acknowledge, say sorry when we mess up, and always be open to feedback.

Leadership is not easy. Compassion is a vital component.

Chris has succeeded in providing a highly engaging mix of life experience, psychology, and neuroscience, along with approaches and insights and where to go next, all in one book. There is a superb collection of diagrams. You will explore the human side of leadership: how to truly understand people and yourself, trust, team development, culture - right through to personal meaning and looking after your most important asset – YOU!

In 2019, some thirty years on from my encounter with Karen, I ask myself, where should this book sit amongst the other books on business, management, and leadership, that now grace my bookshelf?

I think of it as a portal to leadership development, a signpost for where to go next and a compass for leadership thinking.

Enjoy.

Ade Brown
Owner and Chief Executive
VP MED Group

PS. I am off to get my keys for the DeLorean, warm up the flux capacitor and set the dial for 1996.

INTRODUCTION

In my first job, as a trainee design engineer, I had a stand-up row in the middle of the office with one of the partners, Ken Tune. I remember our final exchange. He said "You know what they say, a man's what he is when he's angry" and I retorted "You know what they say, lead by example and if we followed yours we would all be reading the Daily Telegraph all day." I may have deleted one or two expletives from that sentence.

Looking back I'll never know how I did not get fired. But I do know that subsequently my then boss, John Gregory, somehow managed to communicate the boundaries of reasonable behaviour in the business without criticising me. I felt strangely understood – maybe John knew that I was a country boy from Rotherham who hadn't the faintest idea about how to conduct himself in the offices of an engineering multinational.

Maybe he didn't, but the effect was the same - he won my undying respect, and though engineering design ultimately proved not to be my thing, I applied myself as best I could for the rest of my time there.

I wrote this book as a reference for all those managers who share John's vision of a civilised workplace. It is intended as an antidote to those business 'reality' TV shows where respect flows one way, and the big boss gratuitously tears into his hapless charges before announcing "You're fired!" The participants compete ruthlessly with one another, are encouraged to put one another down, and fame and money are the sole motivators.

In my experience, leadership in successful companies is not like that. It's about putting your people first, creating a convivial work environment, supporting individual and team fulfilment, and ultimately giving everyone, including you the manager, a more purposeful and satisfying life.

I also wrote this book because my years as a manager would have been improved beyond measure had I acquired this understanding earlier. As it is, I have built an appreciation of compassionate leadership over a period of 40 years. It was accelerated in my twenties by a year spent as a management academic. During the past two years, when I launched a new career as a coach and mentor, I have acquired the knowledge of neuroscience and psychology that has helped me to reflect deeply on my practice as a manager and understand why some things worked so well (and others didn't).

Gareth Morgan has used the terms 'instrument of domination' and 'psychic prison' to describe some workplaces. This book is about exploring how we might create 'places of belonging'. And as businesses come to rely ever more on the creativity, initiative and independent thought of their employees, compassion turns out to be a fundamental building block of the modern organisation.

Most people are looking for leaders that are authentic, emotionally aware and capable of coaching and mentoring them to success. They rightly have no time for leaders who are autocratic, insecure in themselves and concerned only with their own progress. However, our education system does little to equip students with the interpersonal skills and the understanding of human psychology that first-rate leaders possess.

Our colleges, universities, and businesses seem to take the view that learning is first and foremost about acquiring and handling technical information. The better universities run team projects, but there is very little reflection or debriefing going on. Unless you are taking a course in psychology, students are expected to develop their understanding of human nature, the bedrock of interpersonal skills, in their own time.

As a result, people are often thrust into a teamworking environment with little understanding of how effective teams operate and even less understanding of what might be behind the thinking, behaviour, and the emotions, of their colleagues. This leads to a tendency among managers to treat human relationships as cruising down an eight-lane highway, when in fact they are picking their way through a minefield. They carelessly plough on as if it's a long straight road when in fact it is strewn with obstacles and the potential for lasting damage.

PART 1

We begin the book by considering the complexity of the human organism and its thinking because understanding is the foundation of compassion and people are more complex than we might imagine.

The intention is to provide you with an entry-level understanding of how the human mind works. It is an understanding that started with Jung and Freud 130 years ago and is being enhanced continuously by modern psychology and neuroscience.

The first three chapters – The Brain, The Mind and Body, and Human Agency – cover some of the latest discoveries of neuroscience, the mind/body connection and issues around agency.

In the following seven chapters – Attachment, Transference, Projection, Defence Mechanisms, Personality Disorders, Unfinished Business, and Emotional Bandwidth, Motivational Needs and Addiction – we look at the ways in which our experiences and genetics colour the way we think and act. In particular, we see that a pattern of thought that served an individual at one point in time can become unhelpful at a later date.

Finally – in Transactional Analysis, Theories of Human Development and Systemic Thinking – we take in some useful lenses through which we can view patterns of human thought.

I believe that having an understanding of the complexity of human thought will help you to work with the grain of human nature rather than against it. The rest of the book explores how you might apply this learning to your everyday management practice.

PART 2

Part 2 looks at what compassionate leadership means for our one-to-one interactions. It covers the key skills of becoming self-aware and listening attentively. It draws on the work of two influential therapists, Carl Rogers, and Dan Hughes.

PART 3

Part 3 extends the conversation to teams. Is there such a thing as the emotional intelligence of a team? Why is culture so powerful and persistent? Why is it so important to create meaning for a team? And what the hell is the Duke Ellington Principle?

PART 4

Finally, we get around to the all-important subject of self-compassion. It's actually the basis for the previous two sections: if we are to be fully compassionate to others, we need first to have that compassion for ourselves.

I once worked for an SME that was twice as productive in terms of profit per person than a head-on competitor selling identical services. How could this be? In simple terms it was because its owners, Ed and Tom Westgate, had an intuitive understanding of compassionate leadership: they trusted and respected their employees, they celebrated the diversity of their workforce, and their employees gave their best in return.

It's a viewpoint that Ed and Tom have in common with leaders of some of the world's most successful multinationals, including Richard Branson, Herb Kelleher, and Tim Cook.

I hope that this book helps you to look at people through a new lens, one that sees a wider range of people as 'normal.' I call this enlarging our 'window of tolerance.' Consequently, you may change your approach to the outliers in your business; the people whose behaviour can be hard to fathom at times but whose loyalty, creativity, skills and/or work ethic may be outstanding. I am not advocating a business with no boundaries, but rather one that is prepared to accept a wider range of individuals and, if necessary, work with them to address the behaviours that their colleagues may find problematic (rather than firing them).

Incidentally, in using the phrase 'window of tolerance' in this way, I am conscious that I am subtly adapting the expression which Daniel Siegel describes as "the band of arousal [of any kind] within which an individual can function well." I am using it to characterise the range of personalities, temperaments, and attitudes in others that an individual can functionally interact with.

Out of compassion for you, the reader, I have not attempted to define 'compassionate leadership.' Rather this book is an attempt to equip you for the challenge, in whichever way you choose to pursue it. At the end of each chapter, I have added three key points. These are my key points. If you are taking away something different, feel free to cross them out and insert your own! Similarly, in parts 2 to 4, I have added one thing that you can try straight away.

I have gone for breadth: my aim has been to give you an appreciation of the size of the warren rather than the depth of each rabbit hole. Should you wish to go deeper I have added a recommendation for further learning at the end of each chapter. There is a section detailing my references at the end of the book.

In the book I have used the terms coaching, mentoring, therapy, counselling and supervision to describe helping relationships. In broad terms, the distinction between them is that coaching helps you look at the present as a basis for making decisions about the future. Coaching assumes that all of the answers reside within the coachee. Mentoring is similar but assumes that most of the answers reside within the mentor. Therapy looks at the past as a means of understanding the present. Counselling is similar but is generally short-term in nature. Supervision is a helping relationship between a supervisor and a professional coach, mentor, therapist, counsellor or similar with quality assurance, developmental and restorative goals.

About 8 billion people out there have a different mental map of the world from you. This book is about creating an environment where as much of that diversity as possible is appreciated and celebrated.

PART 1:
UNDERSTANDING THE HUMAN MIND

PART 1: UNDERSTANDING THE HUMAN MIND

THE BRAIN

My Uncle John had the unlikeliest of career trajectories. Originally a bus conductor in Rotherham, he won a Trades Union scholarship to Ruskin College, Oxford, became a renowned authority on the Brontë sisters and their writing and finished up headmaster of a public school.

He and my dad fell out long before I was born – over a fiver that my dad had lent John – and didn't speak for 40 years. Then one day, when my dad was in his seventies, a letter from John dropped on his mat. It was a beautifully written evocation of their childhood together, and it must have spoken to my dad because very soon after that I found myself driving him to Moelfre on Anglesey, where Uncle John was living in retirement.

I watched with a mixture of wry amusement and open-mouthed astonishment as they embraced. And for the next two years, before my dad died, you would have thought they had never had a cross word.

John and my dad were illustrating a key finding of modern neuroscience, which is that the brain remains plastic for one's entire adulthood, so you can indeed teach an old dog new tricks and leopards can change their spots. 'It's never too late to mend' is closer to the truth.

When we think, we integrate inputs from the body, from other people (yes, they become part of our consciousness) and from multiple regions of the brain. So the brain is only one part of our thinking system. However, it is the integrative part, and so we are going to start with it.

First some elementary biology. Information within our brain is held by cells called neurons, which communicate by sending electrical signals across a synapse, the small gap that separates one neuron from another. The average human brain has about 100 billion neurons and many more glial cells, which serve to support and protect the neurons.

The brain has developed in layers throughout evolution, and we can use these to think about its structure.

The Reptilian Brain

The brainstem, sitting deep within and at the bottom of the brain, and made up of the pons, medulla, and midbrain, is our 'reptilian brain.' It receives input from the body and sends out signals that regulate our basic processes, such as the functioning of our heart and lungs. It controls our states of arousal, whether we are hungry or satiated, sexually aroused or relaxed, awake or asleep.

The Mammalian Brain

This part of the brain first made its appearance when mammals evolved two hundred million years ago. It is what Steve Peters calls our 'chimp brain.' It comprises of the hypothalamus, the amygdala, and the hippocampus. The technical term is the 'limbic system.'

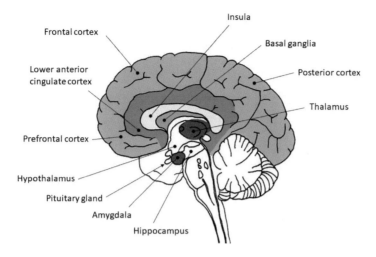

Insula
Frontal cortex
Basal ganglia
Lower anterior
cingulate cortex
Posterior cortex
Thalamus
Prefrontal cortex
Hypothalamus
Pituitary gland
Amygdala
Hippocampus

Figure 1: The brain

The hypothalamus controls the pituitary gland, which dispenses a pharmacopeia of hormones. When we are stressed, it stimulates the adrenal glands (located on the top of each kidney) to release cortisol, which puts our metabolism into a state of readiness to meet a challenge.

To either side of the hypothalamus, we find the amygdala, which is central to our fear response, and the hippocampus, which links together widely separated parts of the brain. The hippocampus combines our emotional and perceptual memories into autobiographical narratives.

Memories generally come in two types: implicit and explicit. As a child, we learn the motor skills necessary to walk. When we stand up and walk, our brain recalls those skills, but they don't come associated with the experience of walking for the first time. They are implicit. The memory has influenced our behaviour in the present, but we are not normally aware that we have recalled it.

Explicit memories are what we normally think of as 'memories', that is they come with an orderly narrative, and we recognise that we are recalling them. By the way, implicit memories are not the same as 'unconscious memories.' The latter are explicit memories that have been buried or repressed.

The New Mammalian Brain

Wrapped around the old mammalian brain is an area that expanded with the appearance of primates and particularly human beings. The new mammalian brain creates a more intricate world beyond our bodily functions and survival mechanisms.

The posterior cortex interprets inputs from our five senses in order to create a perception of our physical position and the world around us. The frontal cortex controls our voluntary muscles and also allows us to plan our actions.

Within the cortex sits the insula, where information is received from our heart, lung, and gut. It generates that sense that we can't explain, but we can feel in one of those organs.

Behind the human forehead lies the newest part of the brain, namely the prefrontal cortex. It's this part of the brain that allows us to think about our thinking, potentially a unique capacity in the animal kingdom, and to combine facts and experiences and thereby create new concepts and ideas. The prefrontal cortex provides our sense of self, allows us to make moral judgements and to respond to others with intuition and empathy.

I will allow myself an aside. Parents of teenagers will be relieved to hear that the part of the prefrontal cortex responsible for empathy is not fully developed until one's early twenties. Phew! It isn't you after all.

Between the prefrontal cortex and the amygdala lies the lower anterior cingulate cortex. This is a key element of our executive brain, the system for regulating our emotions.

Just because we have this marvellously sophisticated organ at our disposal doesn't mean that we use it at all times. Some drugs, such as alcohol, and states of high emotion, such as rage, can impair the functioning of the hippocampus and create memory blackouts. Short of that, high emotion can saturate the limbic system and prevent the onward flow of signals to the cortex, effectively shutting down our higher order thinking.

The Left and Right Sides of the Brain

The left and right side of the brain complement each other. The left is the realm of logic, language, and literal thinking. The right is the realm of creativity, whole body sense and big-picture thinking. The two sides of the brain are linked to one another by the corpus callosum.

Ideally, the two halves should be integrated and balanced, but that isn't always the case. For example, if our early bids to become close to our parents are met with either indifference or hostility we may mentally retreat to the safety of the left hemisphere. Without therapeutic intervention, this can be a permanent adjustment.

Neuroplasticity

Neuroplasticity is the ability of the brain to change, and it is possible because when adjacent neurons communicate, the genes in their nuclei produce proteins which strengthen the links between them. In this way, our reaction to repeated experiences of a similar nature becomes stronger and more automated.

It all happens with our best interests at heart. If the reaction to an experience is functional, then the 'learning' encoded by our brain serves to minimise future effort, which then permits us to attend to other matters. Unfortunately, the converse applies and if the learning is dysfunctional, then the adaptation can cause long-term harm: we may react to new circumstances in a way that has outlived its purpose.

By becoming aware of our thoughts and directing that awareness to change our thinking, we can create new neural firing patterns that link previously separated areas and serve us better. For example, the insula and anterior cingulate respond to experiences in life by either contracting or expanding.

Engaging in compassionate meditation has been shown to promote the expansion of these parts of the brain, whereas people who have been exposed to certain types of trauma may develop an underactive insula, a condition known as 'alexithymia', in which they become disconnected from their feelings. Because they lose their 'gut sense' they tend to lack intuitive knowledge about the internal states of others.

Prolonged exposure of the hippocampus to stress hormones such as cortisol impairs the processes by which neurons proliferate and strengthen the links between them. This can cause poor hippocampal functioning and even structural changes. Such poor functioning and structural change are common features of many psychiatric disorders, including depression, PTSD and schizophrenia.

Emotional Pain

In brain scans, the brain centres that light up during physical pain also become activated during emotional rejection. Social ostracism has the same impact as a physically harmful stimulus. Therefore 'hurt' or 'emotional pain' are not just figurative expressions but can be a more accurate representation of reality than we formerly imagined.

Mirror Neurons

In the late 1990s, a group of Italian scientists discovered that some motor cells in primates and humans are activated by watching an opposite number engage in a purposeful action, including making facial expressions and gestures. The contagion of yawning is the work of the mirroring system, and the system may also explain why anxiety is contagious: when we mirror we feel some of what the other person is feeling.

Daniel Siegel describes mirror neurons as the "root of empathy" and explains that "our brains use sensory information to map out the minds of others, just as they use sensory input to create images of the physical world."

The map we create can never be as detailed as the actual mind of the other person – even the most empathetic individual cannot create a perfect duplicate. Nonetheless, this explains, for example, why authenticity is so difficult to fake. We can pick up when the verbal message is inconsistent with what the speaker is feeling. In coaching or therapy, the recognition of a feeling transmitted in this way is termed the therapist's 'use of self': the therapist is using their own organism as a receiving station for the client's unspoken thoughts.

Key Points

- The brain remains plastic throughout our whole lives and by directing our thoughts we can, over time, 'rewire' it.
- Some drugs and states of high emotion can flood the limbic system, interfering with our memory and shut down our higher order thinking.
- Mirror neurons allow us to observe another human being and pick up some of what they are feeling.

Learn More

Siegel, Daniel J. (2011). Mindsight: The New Science of Personal Transformation, New York: Bantam.

THE MIND AND BODY

One of the most productive partnerships of my working life was with a boss, Alex, who could be a nightmare. On one occasion he insisted I maintain a particular negotiating position with a client and, dutifully following his instructions, I had held the line for several months. Then one day he pitched up at a meeting with the client, capitulated on the point and took me to task over it there and then while the client observed us with some satisfaction.

There was an uneasy silence in the taxi on the way back to the airport, which was broken when Alex said "I am a bastard, aren't I?" – well, you couldn't accuse him of being inauthentic. But the reason our partnership was so productive was that he was predominantly a 'gut' person and I was a 'head' person. He had an extremely well-developed gut instinct and made most of his decisions based on it. He was a moderniser, and it is fair to say that he transformed our organisation for the better.

However, gut instinct did not fly so well with our top management, and that is where I came in, assembling the rational justification for his ideas. Detail was not his thing, and I helped make his vision a reality by paying attention to the finer points.

Some people think of the brain and mind as interchangeable terms. They are not, for two reasons.

Firstly, our thinking system is not limited to the brain in our heads. All the major organ systems of the body include neural networks that process complex information, including our heart, lungs, intestines, and muscles. Some of this circuitry forms the autonomic nervous system, an automatic system that keeps our body in balance, and some the voluntary system that allows us to move our limbs.

Our thoughts can be influenced profoundly by the state of our body. If we deliberately relax our breathing, for example, we can calm the fear circuitry in our brain via the vagus nerve.

Secondly, the mind is not an organ but a process within that distributed nervous system. Siegel defines it as "a relational and embodied process that regulates the flow of energy and information." We can divide the mind up into our conscious mind, which normally operates as if it is in full control of the whole organism (if only) and the unconscious, automatic part of the mind.

One hundred and thirty years ago, Freud expressed the view that the proportion of the conscious to the unconscious mind in our psyche is unequal: most of our thoughts go in our unconscious mind. And this is not a bad thing, as our capacity to process information consciously is limited. The parallel processing of vast quantities of material that occurs in our unconscious is vital to our effective functioning.

Modern neuroscience has shown Freud to be right. The main paradigm shift that has occurred since his time is not in the relationship between conscious and unconscious, but in our understanding of the mind-body connection.

Not only do the neural networks in our organs afford us access to a 'gut feel' for something or our 'heartfelt response' but it is now apparent that our thoughts can profoundly affect our physical wellbeing. For example:

- If our early experience is that the world is a benign rather than a malevolent place, then the genes influencing our stress response will structure our nervous system so that we can adjust to stressful experiences in the future in a more measured way, releasing less of the hormones that can cause long-term damage to our bodies.

- The mind can defend us from pain by dampening the passage of energy and information from the subcortical region to the cortex. Such dampening may occur short-term, when we are overwhelmed, or long-term in response to a significant trauma, such as the loss of a parent in our formative years. This can compromise our ability to tune-in to signals from the body that tell us we are in danger or safety. If we can't detect when we are in a safe environment, then we may waste a lot of energy in a state of alert, when we could be relaxing and becoming more receptive.

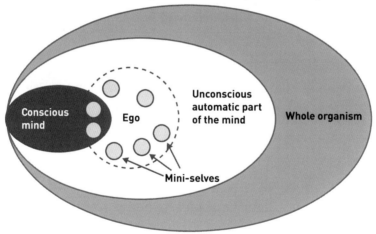

Figure 2: A model of the mind (Bachkirova)

The model in figure 2 above brings the mind and body together and adds two further concepts: a 'mini-self' is a region of the brain that becomes activated when the organism thinks, and the 'ego' is an aggregation or network of mini-selves that translates the needs and desires of the organism into action. The network of mini-selves that are activated will depend on those needs and desires, and therefore the ego itself is in a state of constant flux.

In the chapter on Transactional Analysis, we will see that the ego may recruit different networks of mini-selves during the course of a conversation, with the result that we transit from an adult to a child or parent persona. And in Theories of Human Development, we find that we may achieve different developmental stages in different domains of our life, such as work, family and sex life.

The concept of 'mini-self' can be used to explain the virtue of 'relaxed concentration', also known as 'soft thinking.' When we are concentrating hard, the brain tends to activate the most established mini-selves out of expedience. However, when we use a softer focus, our brain will activate a wider network of mini-selves, and hence more original ideas may emerge.

It's also a reason why a coach's ability to look awry at a situation and probe the periphery is important rather than ask the blindingly obvious questions that the coachee could ask themselves. The left-field question is more likely to stimulate a mini-self that was formerly off-line and may be able to contribute to the ability of the ego to think around a complex matter.

Key Points

- All the major organ systems of the body include neural networks that process complex information.
- The mind is not an organism but a process, involving the flow of energy and information.
- Most of our thoughts occur in our unconscious mind.

Learn More

Bachkirova, T. (2011). Developmental Coaching: Working with the Self. Maidenhead: McGraw-Hill/ Open University Press.

HUMAN AGENCY

I remember my one and only conversation with a careers teacher at my secondary comprehensive school, Oakwood in Rotherham. "What would you like to be?" he asked. "An airline pilot" I responded. "Look, there aren't many airline pilots" he advised me "so your chances of doing that are slim. You're good at maths; why don't you become a civil engineer?"

And so was set the direction of my career for the next 40 years. I am not complaining, as it was a pretty enjoyable career for the most part, but I sometimes reflect on how I went along with it so readily. I suspect it was something to do with the working-class South Yorkshire culture in which I was embedded – aspirations were pretty non-existent, both my parents had an outlook which I might characterise as dutiful: you put up with your lot as best you could.

There was probably another aspect to it. There were plenty of other things going on in my life and so turning over the decision on my future career to Mr. Brown helped manage my anxiety levels.

However, it serves to illustrate a conundrum that has been debated by psychologists for at least the past 130 years: the person-situation debate. This is not a debate about the conscious and unconscious mind – it has long been accepted that most of our thinking occurs in our unconscious. Rather it is about the extent to which we are in command of even our conscious thoughts. Are we masters of our own destiny or are we slaves to the situation for the most part?

We struggle with the latter notion because the sense of control is an important part of effective psychological functioning, yet an increasing number of psychologists are coming around to the viewpoint that we have far less agency than we think. Bachkirova contends "… decisions are being made, not by a conscious, rational agent, but by the underlying [unconscious] processes."

Often we imagine that we are the author of a decision, but in reality, our subconscious has made the decision and our conscious mind has gone along with it. The conscious mind tricks us into thinking that it made the decision.

Self-sabotage is the most obvious manifestation of this. On occasion as a coach, I will hear a client make a commitment to a change in their life, for example, a senior manager committing to more engagement with her team. We may agree the steps she needs to take toward her goal. But after several further sessions, nothing has been achieved.

Whilst the client may be 'committed' on a conscious level, her whole organism, including her subconscious and her body, remains to be convinced. The coachee holds hidden commitments and assumptions that need to be surfaced before tangible progress can occur. In the meantime the coachee's subconscious will concoct perfectly good reasons for avoiding the issue and the coachee's conscious will swallow them hook, line and sinker.

Key Points

- The debate about human agency has raged for 130 years and has yet to reach a definitive conclusion.
- The current consensus is that the unconscious mind is dominant in our decision making, even when we believe that our decision is a conscious one.
- As a result, often we need to surface our unconscious thinking through coaching or therapy before we can make progress.

Learn More

Ariely, D. (2009). Predictably Irrational: The Hidden Forces That Shape Our Decisions. London: Harper Collins Publishers.

ATTACHMENT

I have a friend, Johnny, who is a family therapist and his main role is to explain attachment to foster children and their parents. Almost all foster children have difficulty with attachment, and it means that they are like a ticking bomb that goes off in adolescence. The challenge that this stage of life poses to them results in extreme behaviour for which, without counselling, the foster parents often blame themselves.

Another friend, Mark, who is a foster parent, described it to me like this once. We were on a train to Derby with our bikes, and I asked if he'd like a cup of tea from the buffet bar. When I returned, he said to me "The cup of tea made me think about my foster child. When you asked me if I'd like a cup of tea, I simply answered yes. If you'd asked [my child] it would have started a whole set of scripts running – don't you think I can afford a cup of tea? Do you think I am too stupid to be able to order a cup of tea? Don't I get a say in what I want to drink? What do you want from me? And all you would have done is asked him if he'd like a cuppa."

Of all the theories of human behaviour, attachment is the most foundational. NICE estimate that 30 to 35% of children in the UK have an insecure attachment. Estimates of the percentage of adults in the US with some sort of attachment disorder vary from 30 to 50%.

What precisely is attachment?

In the first preverbal years of life, the developing brain learns a strategy for staying connected to the lifeline that is their primary caregiver, normally a parent. This strategy is called an attachment style.

When infants are frightened, feel unwell, or are under threat their amygdala unconsciously alerts them to stop playing and smiling and pay attention to something that could be harmful. Their face shows signs of distress.

If the infant's parent responds in a timely and sensitive way to his distress, he learns to trust safe people and to count on their care. Daily repetitions of this cycle both protect the brain from prolonged periods of stress and reinforce the child's learned ability to self-regulate. This is a secure attachment relationship where the child feels protected and safe, which in turn allows them to explore their world more confidently.

Now, if instead of responding immediately the caregiver is somehow preoccupied and does not respond sensitively, the child 'up-regulates' their attachment behaviour: they become very distressed and maybe angry and are not quickly calmed when comfort is finally offered. This is an insecure-ambivalent attachment. Adults with this style are constantly scanning their environment for threats – that lack of acknowledgement from the boss means they are already looking for my replacement, my girlfriend doesn't like my beard/musculature/love of football and is going to end our relationship. And the idea of saying 'no' may terrify them.

On the other hand, the caregiver might not know how to respond to their infant. In this situation eventually, the infant gives up and 'down-regulates' their behaviour. They have to deal with their own distress and no longer signal a need for comfort. They may become distant and avoid contact with their caregiver altogether. This is insecure-avoidant. Adults with this style tend to be independent, decide what they should do on their own accord and make the working assumption that they are smarter than everyone else.

Finally, what if the caregiver is frightened themselves and frightening or hostile towards the infant? The caregiver is now the source of alarm, and the infant appears dazed or frozen or draws away when the parent appears. This is insecure-disorganised attachment. Around 10% of the general population but 80% of high-risk infants, such as the children of drug-addicted parents, have this style. Insecure-disorganised manifests itself in the adult as a chronic fear that something bad is about to happen, which can manifest itself as a "why even try?" attitude.

The tragedy is that through a multitude of mechanisms attachment issues can be passed down the generations. A complete picture of the way we are 'primed' for parenting, albeit fascinating, is beyond this book. A brilliant account can be found in Brain-Based Parenting by Dan Hughes and Jonathan Baylin.

In the meantime, you may recall the anterior cingulate cortex (ACC) from the first chapter. In a healthy parenting brain, this region turns on whenever the parent receives a negative facial expression from their child and sets about both regulating the parent's reaction and providing access to your prefrontal region, allowing you to attune to your child and self-reflect on the situation.

In a parent that is anxious or depressed – perhaps on account of their own attachment issues - this system is impaired, which makes it less likely that the parent will respond to their child functionally.

Interacting powerfully with our children activates the brain's reward system, releasing the neurotransmitter dopamine into our nucleus accumbens, the pleasure centre of the brain, which resides within the basal ganglia (see The Brain). But the density of receptors for dopamine (and also oxytocin, a pleasure giving hormone) within our brain depends, in part, on how well we were parented as a child.

Certain types of trauma can lead to an underdeveloped insula, which can inhibit our ability to tune into the internal states of others, including our children.

Finally, the structure of our brain, like the rest of our body, is partially determined by genetics: your starting position will reflect your parentage.

However, like many things in our internal world, we don't have to accept attachment issues as an inevitable legacy from our parents and the inevitable inheritance of our children. If we can become aware of them, then we can seek out help to come to terms with our past experiences and defuse their negative potential.

Key Points

- NICE estimate that 30 to 35% of children in the UK have an insecure attachment.
- The three types of insecure attachment can result in a range of behaviour that, whilst they were adaptive at the time, no longer serve the individual.
- Through a multitude of mechanisms, unresolved attachment issues can be passed down the generations.

Learn More

Hughes, D. & Baylin, J. (2012), Brain-Based Parenting: The Neuroscience of Caregiving for Healthy Attachment. London: Norton.

TRANSFERENCE

Recently I coached Amy, an executive in the financial services industry, who became anxious when an appointment over lunch loomed with her manager. What could be behind it? Was the manager going to announce a rationalisation of the organisation? Would she be made redundant? What would her notice period be? How would she pay her rent? Why hadn't other members of staff been consulted? For two weeks she sat frozen behind her desk with dread.

As it happened, her manager was going on extended leave and wanted to ask Amy to stand in for her while she was away. But the pattern was a familiar one: if her boyfriend failed to text her for a day or two she feared the worst, if the team sheet for the hockey club was late it must mean she had been dropped. Then Amy disclosed that she and her mother had been abandoned by her father when she was nine, and it all made sense.

A male friend of mine who is a coach took on a female client ostensibly for coaching on a number of work-related issues. After several sessions, they were making little progress on the work front, and my friend had noticed a tendency for incidents surrounding the client's recent divorce to creep into the conversation. Half a dozen sessions in my friend realised that the client did not want to make progress on the work-related points at all. She actually wanted someone to stand in for her ex-husband while she offloaded all her frustrations on him. My friend terminated the coaching relationship.

Both of these examples concern transference. Freud termed transference the 'repetition compulsion.' It is part of the human process of making sense of interpersonal events in which we transfer our past experience of interacting with a significant adult onto another in the present day.

If you grew up with mature, functional adults, then transference can save you time and be helpful, at least to the extent you are dealing with mature, functional adults in your everyday life. It's one of those shortcuts the mind adopts so that it can dedicate time to more pressing matters. At other times applying learned behaviour from one situation onto another can be maladaptive, and we need to unlearn it.

This is not so easy because transference is largely an unconscious process. Individuals are normally unaware that they are transferring past experiences and the associated mental maps onto their current circumstances. It feels to them that they are simply responding to the current situation in a rational manner.

Few people are so deeply reflective that they can spot transference themselves even after the event. It normally requires coaching or therapy to help the unconscious become conscious. Once we become aware of how the past is alive in the present, we can spot the learned behaviours and, in time, modify our response.

Key Points

- We all engage in transference but some manifestations of it are helpful and others are not.
- Spotting unhelpful transference behaviours normally requires coaching or therapeutic help.
- Once we are aware of it, we can intercept the counterproductive behaviours and, in time, modify our response.

Learn More

Grant, J. & Crawley. J (2002), Transference and Projection: Mirrors to the Self. Maidenhead: Open University.

PROJECTION

Several decades into my career I had a phone conversation with one of my less favourite managers which culminated in him shouting (mild understatement) down the phone "this is all about your ego." In that instant, I was taken aback and could muster no reply, and in any case (see Handling Strong Emotions) a reply would have been futile.

Later I realised that it was the first time in my career that someone had accused me of being egocentric. Various people had given me forthright feedback on some of my other character traits – often quite painful but mostly, OK almost invariably, accurate - but egocentricity was not something that had arisen, and it hasn't arisen since either.

We always have to be careful in these matters, because our ability to delude ourselves can be impressive – that's why coaches, mentors, therapists and anyone else who can give you objective uncoloured feedback are so valuable – but I am now pretty sure that what I experienced was an example of projection.

Projection is a psychological process in which we attribute unacceptable thoughts, feelings, traits or behaviours that are characteristic of oneself to others. Projection is considered a defence mechanism, a response to a potentially threatening experience that moves it from the conscious realm to the unconscious.

In my example, my manager is anxious about his egocentric tendencies and in particular the potential for them to be recognised by other team members. So, instead, he projects them onto me, allaying his anxiety about his egocentricity being recognised and allowing him to lay off the blame for the situation.

As Grant and Crawley point out, "the concept of projection has been part of human understanding at least since Biblical times when Jesus asked, "Why do you see the speck that is in your brother's eye but do not notice the log that is in your own eye?" (Matthew 7:3)."

Calling someone out in relation to projection is far more difficult than, say, transference. Many patterns of transference are patently damaging to the individual and when they are surfaced the client is typically grateful. Projection though is a different matter. It is not called a defence mechanism for nothing, though the repressed anxiety will take its toll in the long run. Acknowledging it is a highly emotional and intense process for the projector and requires sensitive treatment by a therapist.

Projective Identification

The projection rabbit hole can get deeper! On occasion, the projector can come to believe that the object of their projection really does have the characteristics they are projecting and treats them accordingly. The recipient is then pressurised to identify with the disowned characteristics and to behave in ways that fit the projector's fantasies.

My son-in-law didn't get on with school – he is now a successful self-employed businessman – but his behaviour deteriorated further after he was labelled 'troublesome' by his teachers. Smarter teachers recognise the phenomenon. I am grateful to have been taught by some ridiculously supportive teachers in my time. My music teacher, Reg Davey, was some sort of saint – you can read about him in my online blog (see About the Author at the end of the book).

Projection in Groups

When a group is under pressure, it is common for group members to project their feelings of vulnerability, failure, weakness, and aggression onto one group member. The leader of my coaching course at Sheffield Hallam, Vincent Traynor, put it like this: "when a system is under pressure, it often manifests itself in an outlier."

I once led a senior management team that was under relentless demands from above to 'make the numbers.' One particular member of that team became a regular object of criticism with the other members advising me to fire him. The situation was made still tougher when the behaviour of the individual took a turn for the worse and seemed to bear out their views.

It required a significant effort on my part to resist the lobbying and to unite the group towards a common goal. The scapegoat's behaviour then moderated. I believe this was an example of the group's projective identification coercing the scapegoat into conforming to their projection.

Let me close by reiterating what I said about identifying projection, particularly when you are the object. Before you confidently diagnose every critical remark you receive as projection, ask yourself, your coach, your therapist, your reliable colleague if there wasn't an element of truth in it. It's all about balance.

Key Points

- Projection is a psychological process in which we attribute unacceptable thoughts, feelings, traits or behaviours that are characteristic of oneself to others.
- Projection is considered a defence mechanism as it protects the projector from potentially anxiety-provoking thoughts about themselves.
- Don't be too quick to dismiss a colleague's negative feedback as projection. We can all be masters at self-delusion.

Learn More

Grant, J. & Crawley. J (2002), Transference and Projection: Mirrors to the Self. Maidenhead: Open University.

DEFENCE MECHANISMS

To be strictly accurate, this chapter should be called 'Other Defence Mechanisms' as projection has been covered in the previous chapter: because projection is so salient, I gave it a chapter of its own.

I have a relative, Sharon, whose father told her that she was stupid and would never amount to anything. On various occasions, she has started courses at college to equip her for a better job. Despite receiving positive feedback and good marks for her work, she has been unable to complete a single course. After 40 years she remains in a low-skilled job. She has taken on board ("introjected") her father's verdict on her and has never been able to overcome it.

This is a desperately sad illustration of how powerful and damaging defence mechanisms can be. As a child, it was more comforting for Sharon to think that she was indeed stupid than to face the anxiety associated with thinking "My father is hostile towards me and therefore might abandon me."

Defence mechanisms are ways of thinking that we develop to protect ourselves from fear and anxiety. They reduce the impact of a threatening internal or external experience by moving it from the conscious realm to the unconscious realm.

They typically serve us in the short term but then become unhealthy and unsustainable, blocking our ability to deal with unfinished business, eroding our emotional bandwidth (see later chapter on Unfinished Business and Emotional Bandwidth) and standing between us and successful adaptation to a new set of circumstances.

Here are some common ones.

Desensitisation/Numbing

We all know individuals who numb their feelings through drinking alcohol, and we may have done it ourselves at some stage. Taking painkillers and going without sleep are two other popular approaches. It's also possible to do this by adopting a mental attitude such as 'I couldn't care less.'

Deflection

Deflection is a defence mechanism that is designed to preserve our concept of ourselves.

Common examples of deflection include the person who makes a hurtful comment and then blames the reaction they receive on the recipient being too sensitive, protecting themselves from having to deal with their own insensitivity. An abusive boyfriend or girlfriend may respond to protests with "It takes two," deflecting the blame onto the other person.

Sometimes a person may deflect a positive remark. "That was a great job, Mark." "Oh, I have a great team you know." Perhaps they have been criticised for being self-important in the past, and now they maintain a false modesty.

Whatever the nature of the deflection, people around habitual deflectors typically feel that it is impossible to get through to them with accurate, and potentially helpful, feedback.

Introjection

Introjection is the reverse of projection. In projection, we make the environment responsible for what originates in our self. In introjection, we make ourselves responsible for what originates in the environment.

Introjection occurs when we swallow whole a particular principle, often from our parents. "You must always work hard," "Our family has always been unlucky," "You must not show your feelings." The impetus to introject stems from the desire to maintain a relationship with our caregivers and the associated fear of abandonment.

You can often spot things that you or others have introjected when you hear phrases like "I ought to…", "I should…", "I must…"

Confluence

Confluence occurs when an individual is not differentiated from their environment or another person. The boundary between them and others is blurred.

In organisations a team may lapse into 'groupthink' when the members fear threatening their relationships by voicing dissent. You may hear "We all think this, don't we?" An individual may be confluent with their occupation, unable to distinguish themselves from their job role.

In the short term, confluence can be healthy. It is at the heart of empathy. But confluence as a permanent experience is disorientating, with the individual being unable to distinguish between what he is or feels and what others are or feel. They lose their identity.

Retroflection

In retroflection the individual has given up trying to change their environment and turns his action inwards, bottling up his emotions. To the extent that he does this, he splits his personality into doer and done to, effectively two different people. Then you may hear "I force myself to do this job." "It's no wonder people dislike me because I'm just so useless." The retroflector never gets to express their hurt or anger.

In a group situation, the retroflector is likely to say something like "I am happy to go along with what everyone else wants to do" rather than asserting their own needs.

Here is a useful way of thinking about some of these defence mechanisms.

- The projector does to others what he accuses them of doing to him
- The introjector does as others would like him to do
- The retroflector does to himself what he would like to do to others
- The confluent person can't tell who is doing what to whom.

Key Points

- Defence mechanisms are ways of thinking that we develop to protect ourselves from fear and anxiety.
- They serve us in the short term but in the long term can be profoundly damaging.
- The form of words individuals use can give an indication of the defence mechanism(s) at work in them.

Learn More

Palmer, S. & Whybrow, A. (2007). Handbook of Coaching Psychology: A Guide for Practitioners. London: Routledge.

PERSONALITY DISORDERS

When does a maladaptation become a personality disorder?

There is a school of thought that in the developed world we have a habit of over-pathologising behaviour. Our definition of 'normal' has narrowed with the consequence that an ever-increasing proportion of the population is being diagnosed with one disorder or another. And, to the benefit of the pharmaceutical industry, an ever-increasing proportion of those that have been diagnosed with a disorder are being medicated.

Another view would be that in the present-day mental health is talked about more openly than formerly. Consequently, more people are willing to seek help and therefore more are diagnosed.

And a third perspective would hold that the modern world is a maddening place, with change accelerating, the welfare system being dismantled and work ever more precarious. Communities have been fragmented so that there is an epidemic of loneliness and people no longer have access to the therapeutic conversations they once had with close friends. Therefore is it any surprise that mental health is deteriorating?

I believe that there is an element of truth in all of these. I also believe that not all medication is bad. My friend Toby was diagnosed with anxiety and given medication. He said that whilst he was not happy with being medicated, being aware of the potential side effects, it was the only way he could become sufficiently stable to be receptive to the talking therapy that eventually brought about an improvement.

According to the Mental Health Foundation, 19.7% of people in the UK aged 16 and older showed symptoms of anxiety or depression in 2014, a 1.5% increase from 2013. A third of women (33.7%) and a fifth of men (19.5%) have had a mental health condition at some point in their life, the diagnosis of which has been confirmed by a professional.

Figure 3 is an abstract from the Adult Psychiatric Morbidity Survey 2014. CMD-NOS means "common mental disorders not otherwise specified."

What should be obvious from the foregoing is that at any given time your workplace will have a good proportion of people suffering a diagnosable mental disorder. Some of these will be amenable to treatment, others less so. In some instances, the individual may be high functioning, in fact potentially among your most creative and energetic colleagues. (In a very small number of instances you may wish to give the individual a wide berth. We will come to that shortly – under ASPD.)

There are 200 classifications of mental illness in Diagnostic and Statistical Manual of Mental Disorders, Fifth Edition (DSM-5), a point of reference for psychiatrists. We're going to take a look at some of the most common.

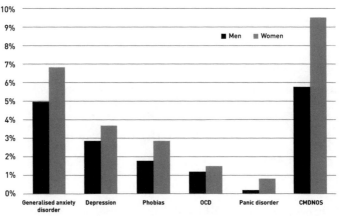

Figure 3: Abstract from the APMS 2014

Depression

Depression is the leading global disability. It is estimated that 7 percent of US adults suffer from depression in a given year. Depressive personalities have a pessimistic view of life, feel worthless and are often self-critical. It is not a passing mood, but a chronic illness that interferes with normal functioning.

People who are depressed may have difficulty concentrating. They may be irritable and suffer from insomnia, and have weight problems and thoughts of suicide.

There are several forms of depressive disorder, including major depression, dysthymia (a milder form of depression), psychotic depression (where depression is accompanied by some form of psychosis), post-natal depression and seasonal affective disorder (SAD). Bipolar disorder, also known as manic depression, is characterised by the cycling of moods between depression and mania.

Generalised Anxiety Disorder

Sufferers from generalised anxiety disorder (GAD) experience chronic worry and tension, often without provocation. They are forever anticipating disaster. Their worries are accompanied by physical symptoms such as trembling, headaches, irritability, and hyper-ventilation.

People with mild GAD can hold down a job; however severe GAD can be completely disabling. It is often accompanied by substance abuse.

Panic Disorder

This involves recurrent episodes of panic and fear accompanied by physical symptoms such as sweating, palpitations, and dizziness. Typically such episodes last 10-20 minutes. Otherwise, the individual will function normally.

Often a panic attack will be associated with a particularly stressful event, such as bereavement or redundancy. The fear of experiencing an attack in a public space can lead to long-term sufferers becoming agoraphobic.

Obsessive Compulsive Disorder

OCD is an anxiety disorder in which people respond to unwanted thoughts and feelings with rituals designed to alleviate them, such as hair pulling, tapping and hand washing. The unwanted thoughts and feelings can range over being compulsively neat and tidy, fearing germs, fearing violence, or having urges to behave contrary to their conscience.

For some people, OCD can be a minor irritant, but for others, treatment may be required in order to allow them to live a normal life.

Paranoid Personality Disorder

Sufferers of paranoid personality disorder are suspicious, distrustful and hypervigilant, always expecting to be exploited by others. They will often misinterpret harmless comments and build up unfounded resentment against others.

People with mild paranoia can be functional in a lone working environment, but find it almost impossible to work closely with others.

Post-Traumatic Stress Disorder

PTSD, only recognised as a mental health disorder in 1980, is an anxiety-related disorder that occurs following an extremely stressful event, such as a sexual assault, physical violence, sociopathic abuse or military combat.

Sufferers may have recurring memories and nightmares, or experience intense replays, known as flashbacks. The latter are believed to be implicit memories of the event that resurface but by their nature are not tagged with a time element, so the individual feels that they are in the moment right now. The sufferer can also feel anxious for no reason.

ADHD/ADD

Attention-deficit/hyperactivity disorder (ADHD) or attention deficit disorder (ADD) is characterised by inattentiveness, hyperactivity, and impulsive behaviour.

It is estimated that some 5 to 10 percent of children suffer from it. According to the NHS, by the age of 25, 65% of people diagnosed with ADHD as children still have some symptoms that affect their daily lives.

Anti-Social Personality Disorder

The French physician Patrick Pinel dedicated himself to developing more humane approaches to the treatment of psychiatric patients. However, nowadays he is probably best known for the observation, in his 1801 paper 'A Treatise on Insanity', that there are some people who look human but are not, in that they exist without empathy or concern for the rest of humanity.

He was describing what came to be known as the 'psychopathic personality.'

Since 1968 the diagnosis 'anti-social personality disorder' (ASPD), or the equivalent lay term 'sociopathy', has been commonly used. However, ASPD omits some of the criteria that are used for psychopathy. For example, psychopaths lack deep emotional attachments, but this isn't necessarily a feature of ASPD. Consequently, psychopathy has become a subset of ASPD – all psychopaths have ASPD, but not all sufferers from ASPD are psychopaths.

Some 5% of the general population have ASPD and around 50% of the prison population.

Researchers Babiak & Hare estimate that 1% of the general population are psychopaths, as are 15% of the prison population and – interestingly from the point of view of this book - 4% of business executives. It is twice as common in men as women.

Narcissistic personality disorder has a high degree of overlap with psychopathy and ASPD.

For the purposes of this book, we are going to use the term 'sociopathy' as a catch-all for ASPD, psychopathy, and narcissism. The common denominators are callousness and low or zero empathy.

Sociopaths don't feel the sense of connection or any of the emotional colour that the rest of us experience. It has been postulated that they engage in anti-social behaviours specifically to fill the void.

Those behaviours may include aggression, violence (though rarely in a work environment), lying and emotional bullying. They often use a practice known as 'gaslighting' to systematically undermine the self-esteem of their chosen victim and cause them to doubt their sense of reality – the practice is named after the eponymous 1940s film, in which a man slowly manipulates his wife into believing she is going insane.

Often the sociopath will deliberately target people who are high in empathy and sometimes they will recruit an apathetic hanger-on ('apath') to aid and abet them. Sociopaths have a knack of identifying suitable apaths.

Sociopathy has the potential to do serious and lasting harm to those who come into contact with it: the victims of sociopaths can experience anxiety disorders, depression, and PTSD. They may become hyper-vigilant and agitated and suffer insomnia and bodily symptoms such as headaches, back pain, and nausea. In part 2 there is a chapter on handling sociopaths at work.

 Key Points

- A third of women (33.7%) and a fifth of men (19.5%) have been professionally diagnosed with a mental health condition at some point in their life.
- Though often a personality disorder will impair the performance of an individual at work, this is by no means always the case.
- Sociopaths don't feel the sense of connection or any of the emotional colour that the rest of us experience. Their behaviour can damage the people around them.

Learn More

MIND (2019). Understanding Personality Disorders. Available at: https://www.mind.org.uk/media/4792976/ understanding-personality-disorders-2016-pdf.pdf

UNFINISHED BUSINESS AND EMOTIONAL BANDWIDTH

I am using 'unfinished business' in the sense in which it is understood in Gestalt coaching and therapy. It comprises of open, unresolved situations which leave one feeling stuck or in a state of regret.

After a 40-year corporate career, I was made redundant for the first time. While I was working through the issues surrounding this with the help of a therapist – could I have done anything to avoid it, had the company's treatment of me been fair, how did it leave me feeling about the company I had left? - a close mountain-biking friend died. He was a drug addict, clean for a while, but then he relapsed and took an overdose of heroin.

Under normal circumstances, I could have coped with his death, but having my recent redundancy in the background took me over the edge. In one workshop session on my post-graduate certificate course, I was being coached and spent the entire 20 minutes sobbing uncontrollably. It actually did me a lot of good, though it wasn't such a great experience for the very gracious woman who was the coach.

It takes time and normally some sharing with a friend, coach, therapist or counsellor to close out unfinished business. In the meantime it serves to reduce our emotional bandwidth, that is the emotional energy we have available to handle challenging situations, seek out new possibilities and fulfil our potential. If left for too long, unfinished business can also affect our health and well-being.

Additional to the unfinished business that can pile up in everyday life are the specific situations created in a work context:

- Role ambiguity – an extremely common source of work-related stress.
- Redundancy, particularly if the reasons are unexplained.
- Death of a close colleague.
- Unresolved episodes of bullying or harassment.
- Any performance issue that is left hanging.
- An ethical dilemma that is unresolved.
- A strong feeling of injustice or unfairness.
- Being falsely accused.
- Having to wait on a decision or event that impacts your life in a significant way, for example, the outworking of a change programme.
- An anxiety provoking conversation yet to happen.

A surfeit of unfinished business can immobilise an individual or cause them to leave an organisation. Recognition of this is why good managers, often with the support of HR, will listen to their staff and attempt to work their way through such issues in one-to-ones, away days and residential retreats.

Some people cope with work-related unfinished business better than others. A pre-existing attachment issue, personality disorder or domestic unfinished business will reduce the bandwidth you have available at work. Individuals whose cognitive abilities are more developed – see Theories of Human Development – will typically have more starting bandwidth.

However, we all have a limit and managerial failure to identify unfinished business and address it comes at a high price in terms of lost productivity and staff turnover.

Unfinished business is also a team phenomenon. Coach Peter

Bluckert observes "Some teams are sinking under the weight of their historic unfinished business."

Key Points
- 'Unfinished business' comprises open, unresolved situations which leave one feeling stuck or in a state of regret.
- It is a team phenomenon as well as an individual one.
- Good managers will listen to staff and work through unfinished business to free up emotional energy and motivation.

Learn More
Bluckert, P. (2015). Gestalt Coaching: Right Here Right Now. New York: McGraw-Hill.

MOTIVATIONAL NEEDS AND ADDICTION

Under 'Unfinished Business', I started to talk about my friend Pete. He had an horrendous childhood. An absent father. An abusive mother who regularly beat him. In his twenties, he turned to heroin and became an addict. Originally from London, he came to Sheffield for rehab, and that was when I met him.

For two years he was clean, and every other weekend we would go mountain biking. They were grand days out, taking in some of the classic trails in the Peak District National Park – Bakewell Circuit, Cheedale Wye Valley, Cut Gate, Five Dales. The scenery was spectacular, the descents exhilarating and the cake stops a chance to catch our breath and have some great conversations.

And then suddenly he was lagging behind on the hills. After a while, he stopped riding altogether. The bike had 'mechanical problems', and then he sold it because he needed the money. He had relapsed, and I lost him to the dark underworld of addiction. While he had a flat, I kept in touch but when he lost that I just heard rumours of where he'd been – sleeping on someone's couch, in a doorway. I caught up with him once in hospital, but shortly after that he took an overdose, and he was gone.

The human being has five basic motivational needs systems:
1. Physiological needs – food, drink, breathing, excretion of wastes, sleep.
2. Sensual needs – the need for pleasure associated with the five senses, including sexual pleasure.
3. Aversion – the imperative to respond to threatening situations by antagonism and withdrawal.

4. Attachment – the need for sharing and affirmation, and for affiliation to groups.

5. Assertion – the need for play, exploration, and independence.

When we are addicted, we take our motivational needs to the limit, using something to the point where it could be harmful to us. Some studies suggest genetics play a strong role in addiction but environmental factors, such as living in proximity to addicts, also increase the risk. Addiction can be a way of blocking out difficult issues and therefore abusive relationships, work pressures, unemployment, and poverty all increase vulnerability.

In the chapter on Attachment, we touched on the nucleus accumbens, the reward centre of the brain. When a stimulus causes dopamine to flow into this area and activate the receptors there, we become attached to that stimulus, which might be drugs, alcohol, sex, status, smoking, gambling, pornography, food, surfing the internet, our children, exercise. Some people might include conflict and personal drama on their list.

Repeated exposure to drugs often results in 'locomotor sensitisation' - increased hyperactivity - due to the chemical impact of the drugs on the structures within the brain, and has been reported in relation to cocaine, amphetamine, morphine, alcohol, and nicotine.

At the same time, the positive symptoms of drug use – such as subjectively reported euphoria, pain-relief, reduced inhibition – typically decrease with repeated exposure. This is known as drug tolerance and is why addicts may eventually overdose.

Prolonged exposure to non-drug stimuli almost always leads

to habituation, that is the amount of dopamine released into the nucleus accumbens is reduced for a given level of stimulus, which might explain why, for example, gamblers tend to seek out ever more extreme aspects of their habit.

Alcoholics Anonymous describes the psychological cycle of addiction as:

1. Pain
2. Using an addictive agent
3. Temporary numbing (see Defence Mechanisms)
4. Undesirable consequences, if any (not all addictions have these, but most do)
5. Shame and guilt, leading to … pain

Berne contended that numbing is only part of the story. He states "Because there is so little opportunity for intimacy in daily life and because some forms of intimacy (especially if intense) are psychologically impossible for most people, the bulk of the time in serious social life is taken up with playing games" and that alcoholism is an example of such a game.

He believed that in the game of 'Alcoholic', drinking is an incidental pleasure. The payoff for the alcoholic is the hangover, which allows the child ego state of the drunk (see next chapter) to be castigated by any parental figures that are willing to oblige and the drunk to self-indulgently castigate themselves. He maintained that Alcoholics Anonymous extended the game by inducing the alcoholic to take the role of rescuer and quotes an instance where the members of an Alcoholics Anonymous group that had run out of alcoholics to work on resumed drinking, apparently because there was no other way to continue the game.

Thus, Berne believed that it was the drama of stages 4 and 5 of the cycle that provided the main stimulus rather than the addictive agent itself. Berne claimed that cured alcoholics are often poor company socially and it's the lack of a feeling of excitement in their lives that tempts them to return to their own ways.

Despite the advances that have been made in neuroscience in recent years, psychologists are still debating whether there is an element of truth in Berne's hypothesis. It's yet another example of the complexity of human thought.

The psychology of addiction is critical to designing social media, gaming and e-commerce internet applications – it is a common joke (though not without foundation) that half of America's psychiatrists are occupied on cases of internet addiction and the other half work in Silicon Valley, advising companies how to design addictive products.

Nir Eyal explains that successful apps depend on:
1. An internal trigger, such as fear or boredom.
2. Sufficient motivation, for example to avoid pain.
3. The process to use the app being as simple as possible.

Whether it's alcoholism, screen time, or retail therapy, few of us can lay claim to being 'clean.' And the consequential impacts on our relationships can be at least as harmful as the primary impacts on our health, alertness or bank balance.

Key Points

- The pleasure centre of our brain is prone to stimulation by a wide range of substances and experiences.
- The positive symptoms of drug use – such as subjectively reported euphoria, pain-relief, reduced inhibition – typically decrease with repeated exposure.
- The psychology of addiction is not lost on internet companies; in fact, it is central to the design of social media, gaming, and e-commerce software apps.

Learn More

Brand, R. (2017). Recovery: Freedom from Our Addictions. London: Bluebird.

TRANSACTIONAL ANALYSIS

Eric Berne was an American Psychiatrist. In 1958, he postulated that individuals have a limited repertoire of states of mind, each of which is accompanied by a coherent set of behaviour patterns. He called these states of mind 'ego states' and categorised them as:

- Parent – ego states which represent those of parental figures.
- Adult – an integrated state which is directed towards an objective appraisal of reality.
- Child – ego states that are a relic of childhood.

The parent ego state has two sides to it; the controlling parent and the nurturing parent. The adult has a single logical and rational aspect to it. The child also has two sides; the adapted child and the natural child. Most people have preferred ego states that they operate in for prolonged periods.

Incidentally, later writers have questioned Berne's original contention that parent and child are replays from the past. It is more likely that we continue to develop these states as we grow and that, for example, individuals that were denied a playful childhood may learn to operate in that carefree state as they get older.

There is no judgement involved here. One ego state is not superior to another, and all can be functional in different situations. For example, the caring professions tend to work in the parent state. Engineers and other technical professionals normally work as adults. Creatives typically operate from their imaginative, liberated natural child.

Berne identified three types of transaction and three corresponding 'rules of communication.'

Complementary Transactions

Complementary transactions occur when the ego state addressed is the ego state which responds – see figure 4.

Complementary transactions can continue indefinitely. There are four channels that have been found to result in particularly effective communication:

Channel	Situation
Adult – Adult	Problem-solving
Nurturing Parent – Natural Child	Nurturing
Natural Child – Natural Child	Having fun, being creative
Controlling Parent – Adapted Child	Giving instructions

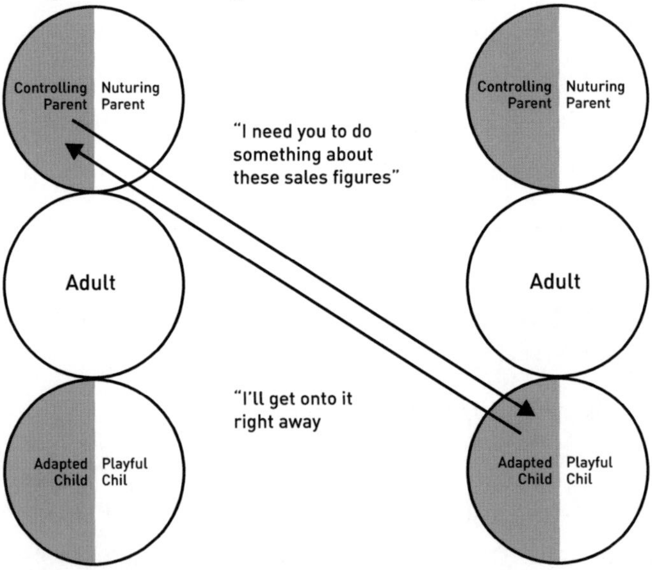

Figure 4: A complementary transaction

Like ego states themselves, each of us has a preferred channel, and we will probably be comfortable with one or two others. Paying attention to the ego state customarily preferred by the other person can give us a good idea of the best way to respond.

Crossed Transactions

Some transactions are likely to lead to impaired communication. For example, if you respond as an adult to someone who is tuned into parent and expecting unquestioning obedience. Figure 5 provides an example.

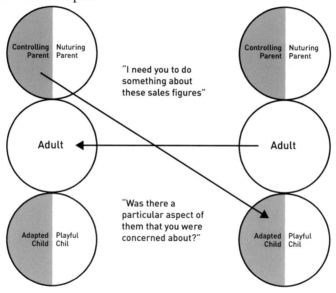

Figure 5: A crossed transaction

These types of transaction are helpful only if you are signalling that you want to make a change to the communication route. And of the course, the other person may or may not be receptive to this.

Ulterior Transactions

These are transactions that happen on both a social (face value) level and a psychological (hidden level). For example, a manager might say: "Let's take a look at the sales figures tomorrow, Geoff." At face value, this is an adult to adult interaction. However, if Geoff is habitually late producing the sales figures, there may be a psychological undercurrent of "Are you going to prepare those figures in time or not?", which is parent to child.

Berne expressed the view that the psychological dimension of such transactions is normally dominant and that unless it is addressed, it will be difficult to build a functional relationship between the two individuals. For example, if Geoff has picked up on the psychological dimension, he might respond "OK. I know I have been late with the figures in the past, but I've set aside time this afternoon to prepare them so that they'll definitely be ready."

Conflict

Conflict normally occurs when one person adopts a particular channel of communication, and the other person seeks to change it, as we saw above in figure 5.

However, conflict can also occur when the recipient of the communication imagines that the originator has an ulterior motive when there is none. If the recipient has sufficient self-awareness, they can employ the STOP process outlined in part 2 to disarm their own defence mechanisms and tune into the ego state of the originator.

Regret-Reason-Remedy

Transactional analysis can help us understand why this formula for handling customer-complaints can be so effective.

Complaint	Let's suppose the complainant is an angry, controlling parent at the social level. There might well be an ulterior communication going at the psychological level where their child ego is fearful that you will not address their complaint.
Regret	First, you need to connect with the complainant. Use adapted child to demonstrate that you are taking their angry parent seriously: "I am sorry that your coffee was cold, Madam."
Reason	Then you can deploy nurturing parent to reassure the hidden child that it is not their fault: "The reason that the problem has arisen is that the temperature gauge was defective."
Remedy	Finally, we can use our adult to solve the problem. "We'll replace the gauge, but in the meantime would it be OK for you if we gave you another coffee and refunded your payment?"

Regret-reason-remedy has been used successfully for everything from lost baggage to major industrial disasters. Incidentally, you might play with it and see what happens if you miss out one of the steps!

Key Points

- Transactional analysis is based on the premise that individuals have a limited repertoire of states of mind.
- Paying attention to the ego state customarily preferred by the other person can give us a good idea of the best way to respond.
- Conflict can occur when the recipient tries to change the channel of communication, imagines that the originator has an ulterior motive when that is not the case or fails to address an ulterior motive when there is one.

Learn More

Hay, J. (2009). Transactional Analysis for Trainers. Hertford: Sherwood Publishing.

THEORIES OF HUMAN DEVELOPMENT

Life-long learning has been a habit of mine, but I have not thought too hard about theories of personal development. I have just got on with it – on my own. And so I have two masters' degrees, three professional qualifications, a postgraduate certificate in coaching and mentoring and a diploma in financial management. With the exception of the postgraduate certificate, these have a heavy bias towards technical knowledge.

I have worked as a design engineer, academic, project manager, bid director, new business director, head of sustainability, head of programme management and MD. I have also acquired a lot of learning by experience.

But despite all this, I wish that I had understood a few theories of personal development earlier. Let's follow the advice of Stephen Covey and "begin with the end in mind." What are we trying to achieve through development?

Much of my training and development was informational: the content was technical in nature and directed at short-term improvements in my performance in role. That is all fine and good. But there can, and should I feel, be a higher order goal to training and development and that is about the complexity of the thoughts that we can handle.

Stages	Unformed ego	Formed ego	Reformed ego
Cognitive style	Socialized mind	Self-authoring mind	Self-transforming mind
Interpersonal style	Dependent	Independent	Inter-independent
	Conformist/ self-conscious	Conscientious/ individualistic	Autonomous/ integrated
Conscious pre-occupations	Multiplistic	Relativistic/ individualistic	Systemic/ integrated
	Social acceptance		
Character development	Rule-bound	Conscientious	Self-regulated

Figure 6: Stages in adult development (Bachkirova)

Bachkirova draws on the work of other psychologists and academics to identify a progression in our cognitive (thinking) style, interpersonal style, conscious pre-occupations and character as we develop. She uses the terms 'unformed ego', 'formed ego' and 'reformed ego' to characterise the three stages of her model, which is shown in figure 6.

In this table, the cognitive style stages are drawn from the work of Kegan & Lahey, who represent them as plateaus in a continuum of adult mental development – see figure 7 below.

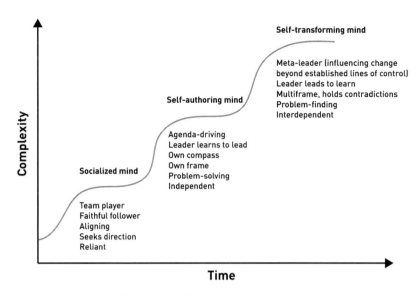

Figure 7: Plateaus in adult mental development (Kegan & Lahey)

In Kegan & Lahey's developmental model, our way of looking at the world becomes more expansive as we progress: what we could formerly only look through (our subject or 'lens' if you like), we can now look at (our object). Initially, we are subject to our feelings, immersed in them, but as we develop, we can detach ourselves and look at them objectively. In the self-transforming mind, we can explore our value system as an object.

This progression is summarised in figure 8.

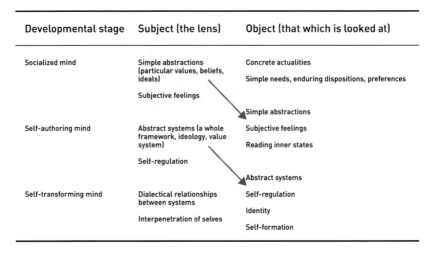

Developmental stage	Subject (the lens)	Object (that which is looked at)
Socialized mind	Simple abstractions (particular values, beliefs, ideals) Subjective feelings	Concrete actualities Simple needs, enduring dispositions, preferences Simple abstractions
Self-authoring mind	Abstract systems (a whole framework, ideology, value system) Self-regulation	Subjective feelings Reading inner states Abstract systems
Self-transforming mind	Dialectical relationships between systems Interpenetration of selves	Self-regulation Identity Self-formation

Figure 8: Subject and object in the three developmental stages

Research has shown that people may exhibit different stages of development without experiencing internal conflict in different domains: sex, work, religion, politics, social situations, and family. This ties in with the notion of mini-selves that we considered in the chapter on 'The Mind and Body'.

Which leaves the question of how we progress through the stages. It won't surprise you to discover that it isn't as simple as deciding one morning that I am going to have a self-transforming mind today. A lot of transformational learning is about seeking challenge and leaning into it. You can find out more under Personal Development in Part 4.

Key Points

- Informational learning increases our knowledge, whilst transformational learning increases our ability to handle mental complexity.
- The socialized mind is dependent on the opinions of others for self-esteem, whilst the self-authoring mind can consider feelings objectively. The self-transforming mind can consider the value system through which we consider our feelings as an object.
- Individuals may exhibit different stages of development in different domains, for example, work, sex, social life.

Learn More

Kegan, R. & Lahey, L. (2009). Immunity to Change: How to Overcome it and Unlock the Potential in Yourself and Your Organisation. Boston: Harvard Business Review Press.

SYSTEMIC THINKING

I have a number of friends who are General Practitioners in the UK National Health Service (NHS). It is an area of the NHS that is under particular stress.

The Head of Health Education England seems to take the view that the problem is one of individual commitment. In an article on 15 June 2018 in the Daily Telegraph, observing that the average GP works a four-day week, he was quoted as saying that "the millennial generation do not want to work the hours done by baby boomers." The implication is that they could work longer hours if they chose to. They simply need to develop a different attitude.

I might question this perspective because I see GPs with a wide range of traits all making similar decisions – to work part-time, to become locums, to leave the professional altogether. Somewhere deep within the human organism, something is triggering a subconscious survival instinct. This is not a matter of personal character; rather it is predominantly a system issue.

The system in question operates at several levels: the local GP surgery, the local healthcare environment, the NHS as a whole and nationally.

At the local level, many GPs are overworked, with practices exploiting the vocational nature of general practice and the consequent goodwill of their workforce by expecting them to work unpaid overtime.

Within the local healthcare environment, the primary care system typically handles 90% of health-related contacts with 10% of the resource available to the NHS. It is arguable that the system requires a redesign so that other pathways handle more cases directly.

The NHS as a whole has become extremely risk-averse, partly as a result of the increasing incidence and cost of litigation. This plays out in GPs being required to issue a letter of apology for the most minor of patient complaints and patients feeling they have a license to abuse GPs verbally with impunity: a GP friend of mine told me that a good day was when a patient didn't swear at her.

Finally, on the national stage, GPs are under-rated. The remarkable progress made in acute medicine in recent years has been celebrated in the press, but no-one champions the role of GP practice in early intervention, managing frailty and keeping people of out of expensive acute hospitals. Politically there are no votes in this.

Recently a GP friend of mine who complained to her manager about her level of unpaid overtime was told: "we can't solve the problems of the NHS." You can't fail to spot the irony. The current generation of GPs is indeed trying to solve the problems of the NHS, but in a way that while well-intentioned is misguided and ultimately self-defeating.

When we think about the behaviour of individuals, we need to take into account the context in which they are operating – see figure 9. Sometimes the impact of that systemic context can be the dominant factor in the individual's behaviour.

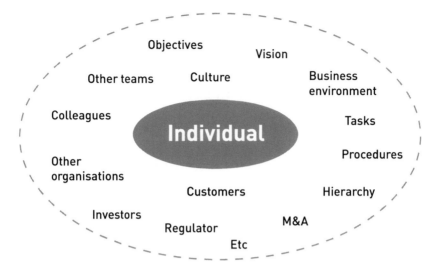

Figure 9: The individual in their system

For example, culture can set invisible limits to candour, creativity, fun, openness to change, respect for the individual and so on.

The characteristics of systems include:

- Changes to one part of the system will directly or indirectly influence the other parts. Hence any part of the system can create stress on the individual.
- All ways of organising the system are not equally effective.
- Left on their own, systems will run down, deteriorate and move towards disorganisation (entropy).
- Energy, resources, and information coming into the system help it to reach a state of balance (homeostasis).

A systems perspective provides us with a far healthier and accurate way to manage error in organisations. The person or scapegoat approach involves hunting for a scapegoat, who can be held responsible for the mess. The systemic view looks for generic reasons why errors occur. Organisations usually have in place a series of measures designed to prevent errors – policies, procedures, checklists, staff training.

The error that has arisen might be the result of a) a flaw within the system or b) deviation from the formal system by an individual or team. However, a systems perspective recognises that such deviation is almost always a result of a problem with the system. For example, in my NHS example, the drop-out rate of GPs is not the outcome of feckless individuals but rather chronic overwork, a litigious culture and a lack of recognition.

Key Points

- When we think about the behaviour of individuals, we need to take into account the context in which they are operating.
- Whilst culture is a key aspect of this, any or all parts of the system can create stress on the individual.
- A systems perspective provides us with a healthier and more accurate way to manage error in organisations.

Learn More

Morgan, G. (1997). Images of Organisation. California: Sage.

BRIDGE INTO PART 2

Management is a messy business unless you aspire to a monoculture, in which case you are missing out on a wealth of talent and creativity.

I have lost count of the number of managers who have said to me "Chris, business would be easy if it weren't for the people." In most instances, it has been said with a wry smile and in the knowledge that it is an absurd statement because people are at the heart of business.

Here is a summary of what I'd like you to take away from part 1.

The mind is an amazingly sophisticated flow of energy and information taking in not just the brain but the whole body and extending, via mirror neurons, to the bodies of people in close proximity to us. The newest part of our brain, the prefrontal cortex, allows us to think about our thinking, which may be a unique capability in the animal kingdom.

However, such sophistication makes us a temperamental thoroughbred as opposed to a sturdy draft horse. We can be agile, creative, imaginative and empathetic but also obsessive, recalcitrant, depressive and manipulative.

We should never expect to find at work a psychologically cleansed group of perfectly-adjusted people. If you do, avoid them, as you would screw them up as soon as you started to interact with them. For starters, we've seen that 30-35% of the population have problems relating 'normally' (whatever that is!) on account of problems associated with their earliest childhood years.

All of us transfer onto others behaviours we have learnt by interaction with significant adults in our lives. And all of us defend ourselves against anxiety by an armoury of defence mechanisms. When we talk about 'pushing someone's buttons' we mean we are threatening those defences. And we all have preferred ego states from which we operate: failure to appreciate this can lead to significant issues with communication.

At any point, the ability of individuals within your team to cope with your pet change project can be compromised by events beyond your control, such as the death of a friend or relative, or events within your control, such as unresolved episodes of bullying or harassment. And at any point, they may suffer from various mental illnesses or disorders that will require sensitivity on your part. For various reasons, members in your team may become addicted and, without treatment, this may have a serious impact on their performance.

Alternatively, the dominant influence on the people within your team may have little to do with you or them but may revolve around the system in which you operate. It's a common error to look for the scapegoat who can be held responsible for the mess. If you're a top manager, you may have to face the fact that you are complicit in a system which is dysfunctional.

The good news is that people of all ages can reflect, learn and adjust. It's rarely a short-term process, but modern neuroscience has demonstrated that our brains remain plastic for our entire lives. Adjustment and adaptation start with you the manager creating an environment that facilitates it, acknowledging any part you may have in your colleague's issues and your colleague becoming aware of how they need to change.

Many of the developmental adjustments that we need to make as individuals involve moving ourselves along a continuum that starts with thinking about things, to thinking about our thoughts to thinking about the thinker.

On occasion, the defences of the individual are too strong, for whatever reason, to allow change to happen. At this point writing them off should be the last option we consider. Sometimes all we need do is acknowledge that their behaviour is not personal, but the consequence of unconscious learnt patterns of thought, and that our view that they have the agency to change them is naïve.

Most companies prosper not because they have a great business model, or great systems, or great technology, but because they have people with a diversity of skill sets working together harmoniously (which takes leadership to make it happen).

Yes, there are some exceptions to this, for example where a business has achieved first mover advantage in a tech field. Even then that advantage can only be sustained by people who are dedicated, enthusiastic, skilled, imaginative, reliable, occasionally cantankerous, sometimes stubborn, often irrational, who get depressed, anxious, angry and suffer loss, illness, and pain. That is life and, as a leader, you are called to embrace it.

In part 2 we will start to unpack what that final sentence means in practice.

PART 2:
COMPASSION FOR ONE ANOTHER

PART 2: COMPASSION FOR ONE ANOTHER

TREATING ONE ANOTHER AS INDIVIDUALS

My introduction to the radical notion that not everyone thinks the same as I do came courtesy of a foreman called Keith Jones. I was a project manager at Eurodisney at the time, putting the roof on the Mad Hatter's Tea Party since you ask.

Our company had experienced payment difficulties with the contractor we were working for – shortly after Eurodisney was complete they went into administration. Anyhow, my team had taken a few days off while I negotiated a satisfactory conclusion. When they returned, I said "Great news, Keith! I have sorted out the payment issues and have told them we will work through the weekend to finish the job." I expected gratitude for my efforts and a degree of relief. Instead, Keith said, "Well that's a shame Chris because we're all going home for the weekend and will be back on Monday."

I was not happy. "OK. You do what you like" I retorted as I went off to explain to our contractor that I couldn't deliver what I had promised.

Later at the airport, Keith offered to buy me a drink. "I'll have a Coke please," I said. "An orange juice please," he said to the barman. "Er Keith, I said a Coke," I said, thinking that he had misheard me. "OK. You have what you like" he joked. My other foremen Steve Thomas and Lynn Smith smiled knowingly, and I had to laugh.

Most people are quicker off the mark than I was to realise the diversity of human nature. My main intention in writing part 1 was to illustrate that everyone is working to a mental map that they have constructed based on their unique genetic makeup and life experiences and that the diversity of thought that this brings may be greater than you have imagined up until now.

With this knowledge, we might learn to respond rather than react on a more frequent basis, ensure we take the views of others into account when we make decisions and generally have a wider 'window of tolerance.' In the words of George Marsden, a former and much-revered boss of mine, "know thy staff." This means knowing more about their preferred style of behaviour at work but also finding out a little – what they are happy to disclose – about their life out of work. You will almost certainly discover things about them that will help you work with them more effectively.

And there is another reason for getting to know people. They are the most interesting part of any job. I have never engaged a colleague in deep conversation without discovering something that has challenged my assumptions about them and, quite often, about human nature in general.

Colleagues of mine have included someone who had been a sidecar passenger in the Isle of Man TT; an ex-professional footballer; a single parent who was raising her sister's children as well as her own and holding down a full-time job; a climber who had conquered Everest; the UK indoor climbing champion; and a director of education who played in a punk rock band in his spare time.

At one company I had a colleague, Harvey Goodall, who had stroked the GB Rowing four at Munich in 1999. As part of a welfare initiative, a local gym brought some rowing machines into the office and created a league table. A friend who was a fitness enthusiast said: "I am going to have to get Harvey off the top of the table." I explained to him that it might be difficult.

In part 1 we looked at emotional bandwidth. Given that knowledge, if you discover that someone has just broken up with their partner, lost a parent or experienced some other form of trauma you will want to allow them a little breathing space.

Towards the end of my career, I started a practice that helped the team get in touch with one another at the start of a meeting, and that is the 'check in.' It involves asking each person to say how they are feeling as they start the meeting and, perhaps, one thing that is going well in their part of the operation. Everyone else listens attentively without judgement or comment.

This practice helps to 'centre' the team and create the ease that they need to be receptive to others. It can be a small step towards a more respectful culture. Some teams add a 'check out,' saying what they have learnt from the meeting, or what they appreciate about a colleague.

Such ideas are not easy to introduce, particularly in a traditional corporate environment, where they may be met with a good deal of cynicism in the first instance. It helps if you start the check-in by being as open as possible about how you are feeling personally. This is just one example of where compassionate leadership involves making yourself vulnerable, a topic we will explore further in the next chapter.

Listening Attentively

It's possible that no-one feels more treated as an individual than when a colleague listens to them attentively. Moreover, good listening can ignite the thinking of our colleagues: Nancy Kline observes that "The quality of a person's attention determines the quality of other people's thinking."

Attentive listening doesn't come naturally to most people. We have been raised in a culture where we are mentally preparing our response while we are half-listening to what the other person has to say, and where we routinely interject and cut across one another during a conversation. When someone comes to us with a problem, our instinct is to try to fix it and we often don't wait for them to finish their oration before we jump in with our advice.

Attentive listening, by contrast, involves listening without mentally preparing our response before the speaker has finished, without judgement and without distraction. It means listening with focus, with eye contact, and with an open mind. The objective is to understand the speaker, not to persuade them of our point of view.

It's a means of appreciating and valuing someone, yes, but it has other benefits.

Carl Rogers said: "I have come to trust the capacity of persons to explore and understand themselves and their troubles, and to resolve those problems, in any close, continuing relationship of real warmth and understanding." If you listen long enough the issue that your colleague has come to you with might just be resolved before you speak.

Additionally, if you listen, you might learn something about the speaker, your team, your business or your industry. If you are focused on putting over your point of view, you have precluded this possibility.

Key Points

- Everyone is working to a mental map that they have constructed based on their unique genetic makeup and life experiences.
- Treating one another as individuals involves getting to know them on a personal level and having a wide 'window of tolerance.'
- Attentive listening improves the quality of the thinking being done by the other person and is often sufficient in itself.

Try This

Start your next meeting with a 'check in.' Give everyone, in turn, the opportunity to say how they are feeling and one thing that is going well for them at work right now.

Learn More

Kline, N. (1999). Time to Think: Listening to Ignite the Human Mind. London: Ward Lock.

AUTHENTICITY AND VULNERABILITY

I would be inauthentic if I didn't acknowledge the extent to which Brene Brown has influenced my thinking on authenticity and vulnerability. An accomplished researcher and author, her 2011 TED talk on "The Power of Vulnerability" had received 39 million views when I last checked and her books; Rising Strong, The Gifts of Imperfection and Dare to Lead, are all classics in the field.

We are authentic when we are genuine and honest; there is no part of us that we hold back. We don't edit our stories, however embarrassing.

It's an orientation that benefits our physical as well as emotional well-being. Inauthenticity requires us to expend emotional energy on those defence mechanisms we touched on in part 1, particularly projection, retroflection, and introjection. And if we keep that going for too long, it becomes debilitating. That said, it doesn't stop people trying, and in some organisational cultures, it has developed into an art form.

Authenticity requires us to let go of what people think - moving beyond the socialized mind (see Theories of Personal Development) - and be vulnerable, as there is always the risk that rather than being reciprocated what we disclose may be used against us.

Brene Brown writes:
"Revolution might sound a little dramatic, but in this world, choosing authenticity and worthiness is an absolute act of resistance. Choosing to live and love with our whole hearts is

an act of defiance. You're going to confuse, piss off and terrify lots of people – including yourself. One minute you'll pray that the transformation stops, and the next minute you'll pray that it never ends. You'll wonder how you can feel so brave and so afraid at the same time."

My experience is that if you as a leader can find the courage to be authentic, others will take it as tacit permission to do the same. In the words of Nelson Mandela in his 1994 Inaugural Speech:

"As we let our own Light shine, we unconsciously give other people permission to do the same. As we are liberated from our own fear, our presence automatically liberates others."

An authentic leader liberates the people around her – Carl Rogers would say they become 'congruent' - and that in turn releases a wave of emotional energy that can be deployed in productive work rather than anxiety and fear.

There is a need to maintain certain boundaries to authenticity: we should not be honest to the point at which we are hurting our colleagues gratuitously. That type of honesty is motivated by our own hurt, anger or fear. In the short term, we need to police it with self-regulation. In the long term, we need to engage in 'shadow work' – dealing with our thoughts and feelings through therapy or other helping relationships.

An organisation where everyone can be authentic is a wonderful thing. People feel they 'belong': they are accepted as they are, as opposed to feeling they have to 'fit in' by sacrificing their individuality.

Brene Brown expresses a view with which I can concur: "The

level of collective courage in an organisation is the absolute best predictor of that organisation's ability to be successful..."

Quite apart from the energy it releases, authenticity increases people's willingness to be candid about the opportunities and risks the business faces and reduces the size of the ZOUD (the zone of uncomfortable debate). Ray Dalio, one of the world's most successful investors and entrepreneurs and owner of the hedge fund Bridgewater, contends "Understanding what is true is essential for success, and being radically transparent about everything, including mistakes and weaknesses, helps create the understanding that leads to improvements." He has made authenticity and transparency the enablers in a business where 'the best ideas win.'

On the bus en route to a workshop with a new client organisation, I was reading Peter Bluckert's book, Gestalt Coaching, in which he describes the swimming pool experiment. The members of a team are asked to "Imagine a swimming pool, shallow at one end, deep at the other. Take a few minutes to think about, then write down four things you haven't shared with this team, grading your four glimpses from 1 – 4 shallow to deep, in terms of the level of risk you would be taking if you were to disclose them to the team. Each person, in turn, shares a glimpse from their list – it can be a 1, 2, 3 or 4."

We finished the meeting with time to spare, so I dropped in this exercise. The team was the newly appointed board of the organisation, and they all headed for the deep end. In fact, they ignored the swimming pool altogether and fearlessly took to the 10m diving platform. That was an inspiring introduction to a business that is thriving, and I am sure will continue to do so.

However, I don't want to make light of the leadership and interpersonal sensitivity required to make authenticity and vulnerability the norm in an organisation. It can be a big ask, particularly if the company is long established and set in its ways. But the businesses such as Bridgewater that have succeeded tend to be way out in front.

Key Points

- We are authentic when we are genuine and honest; there is no part of us that we hold back. We don't edit our stories, however embarrassing.
- Authenticity requires us to let go of what people think and to be vulnerable.
- Authenticity increases people's willingness to be candid about the opportunities and risks the business faces and reduces the size of the ZOUD.

Try This

The next time you get something wrong, no matter how embarrassing, be completely candid about it in front of your team.

Learn More

Brene Brown TED talk on The Power of Vulnerability: https://www.ted.com/talks/brene_brown_on_vulnerability?language=en

TRUST

When I worked at a construction multinational one of the managers marshalled his team under one simple strapline: "We say what we do, and we do what we say." Simple but effective.

Why was it effective? Because trust is such a pivotal issue within organisations. It's at the root of much conflict and political in-fighting. Withholding information and ideas, judging, complaining and defending all stem from a lack of trust.

Many people have developed definitions of trust. I like Charles Feltman's, which ties in with the previous chapter: "Trust is choosing to risk making something you value vulnerable to another person's actions." Thus, choosing to trust involves a risk assessment and a, normally subconscious, comparison of the potential benefit of a trusting relationship versus the cost of betrayal.

There are multiple dimensions of trust, some of which are more significant to people than others. Consider the following breaches of trust.

"You told me it would be ready yesterday and now you are saying another week." (reliability)

"The e-commerce module on the software you provided doesn't work as we agreed." (technical competence)

"He said that he would speak up for us, but in the end, he sold us all down the river to save his own skin." (care for the interests of others)

"She said there would be no redundancies, but already five people have gone." (sincerity)

"Why have you appointed this questionable individual from outside when there were several perfectly good internal candidates?" (judgement)

"Is there any wonder that no-one tells you what is going on when you have a meltdown over such a trivial issue?" (self-regulation)

"I asked you to keep it to yourself, but the whole company seems to know." (discretion)

"He always lets you know his opinions of other members of the team when they are not around." (loyalty to persons not present)

One might argue that breaches of trust that reveal a lack of sincerity or a lack of care for the interests of others have a higher impact than other breaches: it is easier to live with a failure to make a deadline than with the realisation that someone doesn't mean what they say.

However, this distinction may not be as clear as we imagine: trust, like most other aspects of human behaviour, is based not on reality but perception. Therefore, if we believe that the deadline was breached not because of a lack of reliability or competence but because the manager knew all along that the team couldn't make it, then it becomes a breach of sincerity! Trust is coloured by the character, preconceptions, and experience of the observer. We have to face it that what we might consider a minor breach of trust is perceived by others in a completely different way.

Research has shown that the two traits upon which we make decisions quickest when meeting someone new are trustworthiness and attractiveness. In the case of trust, we make our decision using our mirror neurons. We are wired to sense whether the individual's feelings are consistent with what he is saying – it is primarily a test of sincerity as opposed to the other qualities in which we may vest our trust. Our evolutionary success depended on it.

The mind makes most of our acts of trust subconscious in order to efficiently process the dozens of such decisions that we make on a daily basis. Whether subconscious or not, those decisions will be made partly on our 'gut' feel, partly on the basis of our past experience of the individual concerned and partly from our experience of others.

With so much hinging on trust, we need to think about it intentionally. There are four things we can do to improve our trustworthiness in the eyes of our colleagues:

1. Be candid and say what we really think (or don't say anything);
2. Be precise about the commitments we make;
3. If you can't make a commitment, explain why;
4. When we commit a breach of trust, acknowledge it, apologise and explain ourselves honestly.

Managing Expectations

A lot of perceived breaches of trust stem from the original

commitment being unclear, and this goes for commitments you make to both your team and your team make to you.

Suppose your team asks you "When will the new diagnostic software be available?" It's tempting to respond "Oh, it'll be with us by next month." That is so much easier than saying "Well, the board has to sign off the expenditure request first. That is expected next week. And then the supplier has indicated that the acceptance testing will be complete by the end of next month; however, that is a provisional date right now. We have to confirm its compatibility with our security software before we can deploy it. So, the end of June is my best guess."

However, you have been clear on the commitment you are able to make right now and the likelihood of disappointment further down the line has been mitigated.

Similarly, if you need a report from a colleague, "It would be helpful to have a report on the machine failure for tomorrow's board meeting" leaves them to speculate on: Does helpful mean 'essential' or would another deadline suffice? What format and length of report does she have in mind? Is she expecting me to produce it on my own or am I at liberty to recruit the assistance of other members of staff?

Without this clarity, when tomorrow arrives, it is possible the report will be too long/short, lack input from key staff or not be available. You may feel there has been a breach of trust, yet in truth, there has been a failure on your part to communicate and manage expectations.

As both recipient and originator, you need to be clear on the action, the performance standard, the deadline and the resources available to fulfil the request. Clarifying requests in this way will help protect your reputation as a trustworthy leader and the reputations of your colleagues.

On occasion, you will receive requests to which you can't commit. Be honest about it. For example, "I can't tell you how many redundancies there will be as a result of this programme because the end state organisational design is not complete."

Keeping Short Accounts

Everyone has heard the saying "Trust takes years to build, seconds to break, and forever to repair." I would contend that things are not quite as grim as that and that by addressing a breach of trust as soon as possible after it occurs, the damage can be considerably reduced.

It behoves the transgressor to address the breach, though if the breach results in a situation of 'unfinished business' for the person(s) to whom a commitment was made, they too have good reason for raising the matter.

We can use the regret-reason-remedy formula described in Transactional Analysis. For example, "I am sorry that the report I promised you was late, but when I looked into it, I found that George, the machine shop manager, was on leave. I had to wait until he returned in order to complete the report. Next time I will make sure that the resources I will need are available before I commit to a course of action."

Ideally, in this particular example, the commitment should have been revoked as soon as George was found to be unavailable: "I know that I said I would have that report to you tomorrow, but it turns out that George is on leave. His input is vital. Can we agree to extend the deadline until the end of next week?"

Finally, the accuracy of your apology is critical. If it is perceived that you are being insincere in some way, you will be making things worse, a lot worse. For example, if George's absence was not the true reason for the delay, then don't even think about using it.

It may be painful in the short term to bare your soul, but in the long term, it will be a whole lot better: "I am sorry that the report I promised you was late. When I did so, I knew that I wouldn't be able to make the deadline, but I wanted to save an argument. I realise now that I should have been upfront about my capacity to complete it to your original deadline. In future, I will be honest with you."

Post Script

I had an appraisal once, and the verdict of my manager was "You have a tendency to trust people too much." I replied "I can't afford not to because I rely on the creativity, initiative, and industry of the people in my department. If I micro-manage them, I will lose so much imagination and goodwill. So I trust them until I find they can't be trusted, and then I give them a second chance, or two." I stand by that position: the price of widespread mistrust is too high to pay.

Key Points

- Trust is a pivotal issue within organisations and at the root of much conflict.
- Managing expectations is a critical skill if you want to be known as trustworthy.
- If all else fails, keep short accounts. Don't allow a betrayal of trust to fester, but face it head-on.

Try This

Resolve never to make promises that you can't be sure of keeping or don't have the authority to make.

Learn More

Feltman, C. (2009). The Thin Book of Trust. Oregon: Thin Book Publishing Company.

CARL ROGERS

Carl Rogers is an American who is credited as one of the founding fathers of clinical psychology and the person-centered approach. Developed in the forties and fifties, this approach holds that people are their own best experts, and stands in contrast to psychoanalysis where the professional tends to be in the driving seat.

Rogers believed that the role of the therapist is to create certain core conditions for the client. If you provide these then they will thrive, and there is a strong likelihood they will reach their potential; much like a tree will only grow with certain conditions in place, such as sunlight and water.

Roger's three core conditions were empathy, congruence and unconditional positive regard.

Empathy

This is an ability to understand and feel the perspective of the other person. Empathy that isn't felt tends either not to be empathy or very limited. Genuine empathy is a profound connector between people. It generally requires a high quality of eye contact, stillness and listening. It may help if one can find an experience similar to the other person's within one's own memory bank.

I find it easy to empathise with people who need a high degree of autonomy to thrive because I'm like that. I have to acknowledge that I find it less easy to empathise with people who expect regular direction from their manager and who struggle with ambiguity.

Congruence

Congruence concerns the alignment between the client's actual experience of life and their ideal self. If a person's ideal self is incongruent with his real feelings and experiences, he may use defence mechanisms such as denial or repression in order to feel less anxious about the difference.

The role of congruence in our psychological well-being explains why individuals come to think of some work environments as Gareth Morgan's 'psychic prison' (see Introduction) - they find it impossible to be themselves at work – and why so many of them have a mid-life crisis and leave their big corporate for a more convivial SME or self-employment.

Unconditional Positive Regard

UPR involves genuine acceptance of the other person, choosing to see the best in them and seeking common ground. This isn't the same as agreeing with everything they think or say but finding a way of not making judgements. The part of our brain that is responsible for being open to a relationship with another person begins to shut down if it detects judgement.

Rogers contended that in general these core conditions are only rarely encountered and therefore the experience of these conditions can have a significant impact on the individual.

I believe Rogers' work is relevant to management too. It is risky for a team member to share something that is normally part of their private inner world. If it is not received and understood it can be very deflating. Rogers went so far as to say that some individuals that are repeatedly misunderstood will go on to become psychotic, retreating into their own world.

The converse applies, however. If as a manager you develop the skills necessary to create the three conditions and you allow your team members time to explain themselves, they will flourish. And you will deepen your relationships with them, which, if you are a compassionate leader, will make your own work so much more satisfying.

The Johari Window

This is a model that sits alongside the work of Rogers. In particular, it is relevant to the congruence element of the model. I used to share it with all new starters to my department, to help them think about the value of and behaviours around feedback and disclosure.

Disappointingly, its exotic-sounding name is purely the concatenation of the first names of the two psychologists that came up with it, Joseph Luft and Harrington Ingham.

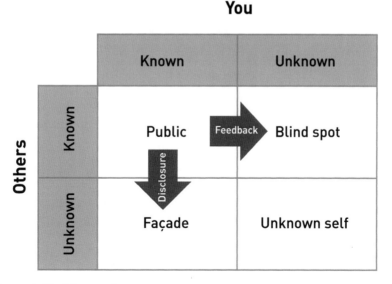

Figure 10: The Johari window

It is based on the straightforward notion that we work together more effectively if we understand more about one another, not those aspects of our private life that we may rightly wish to remain private but the aspects of our beliefs, character, and behaviour that touch on how we are at work. Thus, the objective is to expand the area in figure 10 labelled 'Public.'

We do this through self-disclosure and by soliciting feedback. For example, I knew from a 360-degree exercise I had done once that my delegation skills left a bit to be desired. In fact, a close colleague wrote, "Chris marches down the office with a pile of work, gives you a less than adequate explanation of what is needed and then disappears as quickly as he came." I had tried to improve but I used to share this with new starters and give them permission to challenge this behaviour in me should I lapse.

Equally, I have always underlined to my colleagues the value of feedback to me. If someone had come from a business with an autocratic culture they often found this hard to believe. Even in the most benign environment, people are reluctant to share negative feedback for fear that there will be 'repercussions.' To counter this, you have to be seen to be thankful for and to reward feedback, ideally in a public setting.

Accurate feedback is crucial to our learning and growth and ultimately to becoming more congruent, highlighting for us where our behaviour is not consistent with our ideal self. This means of course that receiving such feedback may not be comfortable in the first instance. As Ridderstråle and Nordström observe, "The truth will set you free, but first of all it may well piss you off."

Key Points

- Rogers believed that the role of the therapist is to create an environment of empathy, congruence, and unconditional positive regard.
- Those same conditions can help individuals thrive at work.
- The Johari window is a concept that helps one think about self-disclosure and feedback, key elements of congruence or being genuine with the other person.

Try This

Share the Johari window with your team and let them know that you value constructive feedback on your behaviour and performance.

Learn More

Rogers, C. (1980). A Way of Being. New York: Mariner.

PACE

PACE is a model developed by Dan Hughes to assist adults in supporting a child's development. In particular, it is concerned with self-awareness, emotional intelligence, and resilience. It is based on a deep respect for a person's experiences and their inner life.

PACE stands for Playful, Accepting, Curious, Empathetic.

The model has an affinity with the work of Carl Rogers. In particular, the empathy strand is the same and acceptance is closely aligned to unconditional positive regard.

Though the model was developed with children in mind, I think it is readily extensible to management. If we want to support the development of our team members, then PACE offers some clues.

Playfulness

Playfulness is not the 'banter' that one hears in some offices, that while amusing to some may actually be a thin disguise for bullying. Instead, it's about suspending judgement and criticism, adopting a light tone of voice and showing interest.

You are looking to create something like the parent-infant interaction when both are just happy to be with one another and are feeling safe and relaxed.

A playful stance can diffuse a difficult or tense situation, provided its use is appropriate, and that is a matter for your judgement and empathy. The better you know someone, the easier it is to become playful without showing a lack of respect for them or their feelings. It's not appropriate when strong emotions are being expressed, though it may be in their aftermath – see the following chapter on Handling Strong Emotions.

Being playful encourages your colleagues to reciprocate with playfulness, helping to keep a matter in perspective and avoiding defensiveness.

Acceptance

Unconditional acceptance is at the core of the child's sense of safety, and it's no different at work. Acceptance means acknowledging the feelings and thoughts, the inner life of your colleagues without judgement.

This does not mean accepting their behaviour, which may be harmful to another person or to themselves: like a parent a manager may need to be firm in setting boundaries and addressing dysfunctional behaviour. The objective is for the individual to comprehend that it is their behaviour that is not acceptable, not them as a person.

In the Introduction, I describe how, despite my inappropriate behaviour, my first boss communicated a profound feeling of being accepted to me. Later on, as a managing director, I found myself having to address a complaint concerning the behaviour of one of my managers, a complaint that proved unfounded but could have been career threatening. During that investigation, I hope that he felt the same grace that I had done 40 years previously.

Incidentally, there is a postscript to the incident with the partner that I described in the Introduction. Some years later, when I was working for a different organisation and after I had learnt some sense, I looked him up and went and apologised. It's never too late!

Curiosity

Curiosity is about getting to know our staff, using a quiet non-adversarial tone. It's not "Why did you do that?" but "What do you think was going on there?" It can help the individual, as well as the manager, become aware of their thinking and reflect upon the reasons for their behaviour.

Crucial to curiosity is the intent. The manager should set out to understand and help the individual, not to spot the error in their thinking and point it out to them. In turn, the individual may come to recognise their behaviour does not reflect something bad inside them, but that they had felt anxious or stressed and had reacted to that feeling.

There is another very good reason for maintaining curiosity in the face of challenging behaviour, and that is your questions might reveal that you have played a major part in the situation! In which case, make sure you acknowledge the same, apologise and learn the lessons.

Empathy

Empathy is covered under Carl Rogers in the previous chapter.

In showing empathy you are demonstrating that you know how difficult an experience is for the other person, but together you are going to get through it.

The Role of Self-Awareness

Of course, the work of Rogers and Hughes sounds great in theory. Applying it crucially takes self-awareness and regulation on the part of the manager.

Firstly you need to be able to give your colleague your wholehearted attention. I have a habit of becoming immersed in my work and can focus on a computer screen for hours on end. But I have developed an inner voice that speaks to me whenever I become aware of someone approaching my workstation: "Move your gaze away from that screen and prepare to give this person your undivided attention." I am hopeful that you don't find it quite so difficult but somehow you need to put down what you are doing, both physically and mentally.

Secondly, you need to be able to relax. Maybe you were quite stressed, working on a challenging task to a tight deadline. But now you need the ability to centre yourself. I have found my yoga practice enables me to take a couple of slow, deep breaths and become present. Quickly scanning your body and relaxing the parts that are tense can have the same effect. Regular meditation can help you develop the capacity to become detached from your thoughts, viewing them objectively rather than being subject to them. In this way, you operate from the self-authoring stage of cognitive development that I described in part 1.

Finally, you need to set the tone mentally. One of the nice things about PACE is that it is so easy to memorise. Sometimes it helps to recall the four words for which it stands before starting a conversation.

STOP

This is a useful model to use alongside PACE. The first of the four stages is critical; where we disarm our own defence mechanisms and create for ourselves space to think.

Stop	Become self-aware and relax, take notice.
Think	Detach yourself and think, zoom out.

Options	Review your options and develop a coherent plan.
Proceed	Respond with PACE, propose a course of action, execute.

Key Points

- Although originally designed to help adults in supporting a child's development, the PACE model can be used to help support the development of our team members.
- The mnemonic stands for playfulness, acceptance, curiosity, and empathy.
- Applying it requires self-awareness and regulation.

Try This

The next time you face a tense or difficult situation, relax and deploy PACE.

Learn More

Golding, K. & Hughes, D. (2012). *Creating Loving Attachments: Parenting with PACE to Nurture Confidence and Security in the Troubled Child*. London: Jessica Kingsley.

HANDLING STRONG EMOTIONS IN OTHERS

When we are in survival mode it is almost impossible to be open and receptive to others: as we saw in the chapter on the brain, strong emotions can saturate the limbic system and prevent the onward flow of signals to the cortex, effectively shutting down our higher order thinking.

That is why if a colleague is overwhelmed by anger or another strong emotion, we shouldn't try to reason with them. Rather we should provide a 'safe container' within which they can express their emotion and then wait until their higher-level thinking is restored.

Once their higher-level thinking has been restored, we can acknowledge the event by summarising in their words what they said. Pretending it didn't happen is disrespectful and, depending on the person, it may also reinforce a false belief in them that they and their opinions don't matter.

Summarising also allows us to check our understanding of the issue. Do it tentatively, because even if you use their words, it is possible that in the heat of the moment they have not been able to express themselves accurately, and you receive the response "No, that's not what I meant at all."

What we do next depends on the quality of the relationship that we have with the person and the trust they have in us. If it's a new relationship, then the sensible option is to give the person space and time to reflect – which they might choose to do with someone they are closer to – and then return to the discussion in a few days.

If, however, it's a longstanding and trusting relationship, then the aftermath of an outburst of emotion can be an opportunity for you to understand one another better. Ask questions to clarify the issue and how it makes the person feel. We're looking for a step beyond anger here – shamed, belittled, ignored?

Use empathy to communicate that you understand how your colleague feels. Validate his feelings – they are perfectly reasonable given his point of view. And then explore what your colleague would propose to do about the situation. Handling strong emotions is a special example of the acceptance, curiosity and empathy elements of PACE at work.

Finally, consider your own role in the situation. If you have played a part then acknowledge it and apologise.

Bereavement

The emotion of grief is one that requires particularly sensitive handling. I'm going to replicate here the advice that I gave one of my client organisations when a member of staff died suddenly:

1. Acknowledge the situation you are in both internally and, as appropriate, externally - we have lost our colleague, and we are in mourning.
2. Emphasise to the team that it's OK to be touched by grief and it's healthy for team members to share their feelings.
3. Accept that people will need to express their sorrow and/or anger. Create a space in which people feel safe in doing so.
4. Recognise that everyone will progress through the stages of grief - denial, anger, bargaining, depression, acceptance - at a different pace. See also Leading Organisational Change under Acknowledging Loss in part 3.
5. Work can be part of the coping mechanism, but obviously

people won't perform at the same level for a period.

6. Provide everyone with an opportunity to celebrate the life of the person who has died. It's part of the mourning process. The funeral will be one such opportunity. You might want to consider whether you provide staff with a further opportunity to remember them.

7. Consider offering grief counselling to staff from an appropriately qualified counsellor.

Key Points

- Provide a 'safe container' within which the person can express their emotion and wait until their higher-level thinking is restored.
- If it's a longstanding and trusting relationship, we can use PACE to explore the situation and our colleague's feelings.
- If you have played a part in the situation acknowledge it and apologise.

Try This

The next time someone expresses a strong emotion at work, wait until they are capable of thinking before you respond.

Learn More

Daniel J. Siegel (1999). The Developing Mind: How Relationships and the Brain Interact to Shape Who We Are. New York: The Guilford Press.

MANAGING UPWARDS

How can we manage upwards with compassion for our manager and ourselves?

Influencing Upwards

Let's start this section by remembering that we are unique, and so is our boss. Our respective mental maps of the world are going to have been coloured by our genetics and our life experiences.

So, influencing upwards is no different from influencing sideways or downwards. It starts with understanding. Before you race into the office of your new boss with that 50-page proposal for a new strategy, get to know him. For example:

- Is he left brain dominant, right brain dominant or fairly well integrated?
- How authentic is he? If he is inauthentic, then it will take you several months of careful observation to discover where his priorities really lie.
- Is he impulsive or considered?
- Does he think detail or big picture?
- How open to new ideas is he?
- What is his family background and what are his interests?

Williams & Miller identified five distinct categories of executive and five associated ways of influencing. Their work was based on a survey of 1,684 individuals. Figure 11 summarises their findings.

Of course, pattern recognition is one of the preoccupations of us humans and the multivariate statistical analysis techniques used by researchers takes this to another level. In truth, Williams & Miller encountered 1,684 categories of executive, each of whom requires a different approach. However, their findings are thought-provoking and illustrate the extensive repertoire of approaches that the emotionally intelligent manager needs in their toolkit.

Category	Characteristics	Approach
Charismatics (25% of survey)	Enthusiastic, captivating, talkative, dominant	Fight the urge to join in the charismatic's excitement. Make simple and straightforward arguments. Use visual aids to stress the features and benefits of your proposal.
Thinkers (11%)	Cerebral, intelligent, logical, academic	Have lots of data ready – market research, customer surveys, case studies, cost-benefit analyses. They want to understand all perspectives of a given situation.
Sceptics (19%)	Demanding, disruptive, disagreeable, rebellious	You need as much credibility as you can garner. If you haven't established enough clout with a sceptic, gain an endorsement from someone the sceptic trusts.
Followers (36%)	Responsible, cautious, brand-driven, bargain-conscious	References and testimonials are big persuading factors. They need to feel that they are making the right decision, specifically that others have succeeded in similar initiatives.
Controllers (9%)	Logical, unemotional, sensible, detail-oriented, accurate, analytical	Your argument needs to be structured and credible. The controller wants details, but only if presented by an expert. Don't be too aggressive in pushing your proposal. Give her the information she needs and hope that she will convince herself.

Figure 11: Influencing styles

'Bad' Bosses

We have been talking about our window of tolerance a lot, and one of my primary goals has been to widen that for you. However, you may say some bosses would struggle to get through a window the size of Macy's in Herald Square. Untrustworthy, moody, incompetent, partial, over-critical, hypocritical, arrogant, intimidating.

I am going to be honest. I have had a very fortunate working life, and the number of 'bad' bosses I have had can be counted on the fingers of one hand, in fact, I wouldn't get past the index finger. So, if I say "Be patient" with your bad boss, you can justifiably say to me "Who are you to say that?"

But see what you think about the rest of the chapter.

Firstly, look at the way you are thinking. The worst thing you can do is ruminate over the situation, dwelling on the negatives. As we have seen, that is a sure route to depression and anxiety.

Consider some of the patterns of thinking discussed in part 1. Could it be that you are transferring your behaviour towards a significant adult that you encountered earlier in your life onto your boss? Are you projecting an undesirable trait that you possess yourself onto them? Perhaps you are responding as a child to his adult ego state.

Secondly, think hard about your own performance. Have you been through a 360-degree assessment lately? If not request one, and in the meantime ask a few reliable friends how they think you might improve. If that doesn't turn up some clues, then lean into the situation and ask your boss directly.

It's always possible he may be perfectly happy with your performance but has issues of his own. I know it's a radical proposal, but have compassion for your boss. He may be a hardworking/workaholic individual who has served at executive level for a long time and, in the absence of a self-care agenda (see chapter on Personal Resilience) has erected defences of numbing and retroflection that have contributed to his current state. He may suffer from depression. I am not encouraging you to psychoanalyse him but to open your window of tolerance still wider and see if it can't take him in.

On the other hand, he may constructively outline some areas for improvement. Don't argue with him. Consider the Thomas theorem: "If men define situations as real, they are real in their consequences." So, assuming he has given you an honest account of his perception of your shortcomings, you then need a plan for modifying your behaviour to help change that perception.

Reflect on what is actually within your control – see Your Locus of Control in part 4 for more details. What can you actually do in practical terms to change the perception of your boss and improve the situation?

I'll leave you with a couple of thoughts that may help you with being patient. Firstly, one of my favourite bosses of all time, Mike Archbold, pointed out to me that "Nothing is forever" whilst an old Japanese proverb put it more poetically: "If you wait by the river long enough, the bodies of your enemies will float by."

I've finished with some black humour. You occasionally need that with a bad boss.

Key Points
- Recognise every boss is unique and that influencing them starts with understanding them.
- Before you write off a 'bad boss' consider your own patterns of thought and behaviour.
- If your boss perceives there to be shortcomings in your performance in some areas consider what you can do within your locus of control to change that perception.

Try This

Answer the questions at the start of the chapter in relation to your boss, and ask yourself if you are using the appropriate influencing style. Check your findings with a colleague.

Learn More

Williams, G. & Miller R. (2002). Change the Way You Persuade. Harvard Business School Publishing Corporation.

MANAGING INDIVIDUAL PERFORMANCE

Some Basics

Because you are reading this book and are therefore interested in leading compassionately, you won't need reminding that if you give someone five times as much positive feedback as negative, then they will normally perceive it as around 50/50. This is because humans are more attuned to risk and loss than we are to opportunity and reward. And for the reasons we have seen in part 1, some individuals will be still more sensitive to negative feedback than this.

So, please be careful and in any event read 'Equipped to Succeed' below before any words pass your lips. If and when you do offer negative feedback, review the result and not the person, acknowledging that it is 'our' result, a result that we have co-created, rather than 'your' performance.

Equipped to Succeed?

I was coaching a director of a social housing business once, and he was complaining about the behaviour of one of his direct reports. "All Simon does is act as a go-between," he said. "He represents the opinion of his team to my senior management team and then apologises to his team for decisions made by the senior management team. I need him to contribute to the top team and to own and explain our decisions rather than grumble about them."

"So here's a question," I said. "Has Simon been equipped to succeed? It sounds as if he may have had very little coaching, mentoring or training before he was appointed to a leadership position." My client stopped short. "Hmm," he said. "Now you put it that way…"

When it comes to performance discussions our starting point should always be unconditional positive regard – our colleague is doing the best they can under the circumstances that present themselves. Virtually everyone comes to work with the intention of doing a good job.

So, the first and most important question is always "Have they been equipped to succeed?" By that I mean, not only have they been appropriately trained, but do they have the right equipment and experience? Are they receiving the support and co-operation they need from their co-workers? Do they understand the mission and strategy of the business? Is their role clear? Sometimes even if their formal role is clear enough you will find that they are taking other roles, for example when team members are absent.

Most performance discussions conclude somewhere along this line of enquiry. Somewhere the individual has not been equipped to succeed and the role of management is to work with them to remedy that.

In the rare event that the discussion doesn't conclude at this stage then the manager should draw on the material in the rest of the book. Is there something that is flooding their emotions and disabling their thinking such as anger, grief, or fear of change? Are they being bullied or otherwise abused? Are they depressed or anxious? Is their behaviour the outcome of transference?

I have a coaching client who suffers from misophonia – it's a disorder in which certain sounds, such as chewing food or clicking a pen, trigger extreme emotional or physiological responses. She is a creative and highly productive operations manager under normal circumstances, but the prospect of moving from her cellular office to an open plan one terrified her.

Rather than disclose her problem to her colleagues, she was contemplating sitting at her open-plan desk pretending to work and then taking her work home and doing it there. I helped her come around to the idea that she needed to share her condition with her colleagues. She did so, retained her cellular office, and the business retained her enthusiasm and application.

Not every such difficulty can be surfaced by a manager or coach. Sometimes therapy is required. Many businesses now recognise that offering a course of therapy to a member of staff temporarily disabled by a mental health issue is both a more compassionate solution and cheaper than spending the money on recruiting a replacement.

Appraisals

I provided some training in appraisals a while ago and realised, as we debated the name of the process, how loaded the word 'appraisal' can be, with its connotations of judgement. Its US equivalent, 'performance evaluation' has an even harder edge to it.

'Performance and development review' ("PDR") is my preferred title, though if we are going to discuss development, then surely performance is going to come up anyhow. So, would 'developmental discussion' be better, achieving the emphasis that most businesses rightfully place on the progression of the individual?

One distinction that the appraisal should acknowledge is between what Ronald Heifetz calls 'technical' versus 'adaptive' challenges – see also Personal Development. The skill set for technical challenges, such as learning how to use a particular software application, is generally well known, and the challenge can be met by the majority of people given a reasonable degree of effort. There's no reason why a development programme shouldn't include half a dozen of these if time and training budget permit.

Adaptive challenges, on the other hand, involve a change of mindset, requiring you to advance to a more sophisticated stage of mental development. Examples are being more receptive to new ideas or being more open to delegating. They normally require coaching or mentoring input (internal or external) and therapy even on occasion. In my experience, it is not a good idea to include more than one of these at a time in a PDR unless the appraisee can expect intensive coaching input.

PDRs are a two-way process. Just as you are reviewing the appraisee, the appraisee is reviewing your skills as a manager and the culture of the organisation in which you both work. As an appraisee at one company, my dominant thought was "I am out of here." So perhaps 'appraisal' is the most appropriate term after all, but not for the reason the manager might imagine.

Here are three questions I always asked myself as a manager before conducting an appraisal:

- In what frame of mind would I like the appraisee to leave this meeting?
- Do I and the appraisee understand the role that the organisation expects of them?
- What questions do I need to ask in order to obtain useful feedback on my own performance?

Key Points

- Every performance discussion should start from the premise that the individual wants to do a good job.
- The first fundamental question is "Has this person been equipped to succeed?"
- In appraisals, the manager needs to appreciate the difference between technical and adaptive challenges.

Try This

Choose someone you believe is underperforming and ask yourself if they have been equipped to succeed.

Learn More

Heifetz, R. & Laurie, D. (2001). The Work of Leadership. Harvard Business Review. December 2001. pp37-47.

THE LEADER AS COACH

If we're committed to the emotional wellbeing of our team, to providing them headroom and to their development, then we could do worse than adopt a coaching style of leadership. This goes beyond the performance discussions of the previous chapter to embrace almost all aspects of the manager's role.

Building on the work of Myles Downey, the model in figure 12 summarises the line manager's role. While there is a circle named 'coaching', where a coaching style ought to be the default, a coaching orientation can and should extend into the other two arenas.

The leader as coach adopts the assumptions that the ideas of his team are at least as good as his own, that collaborative working generally yields more effective solutions than an individual working alone can devise. He believes that shared decision making will generate a high level of motivation and by listening intently and deploying incisive questions, he can improve the quality of the thinking of his team both individually and collectively.

The leader as coach reflects a move from a command and control approach to a more participative style of management.

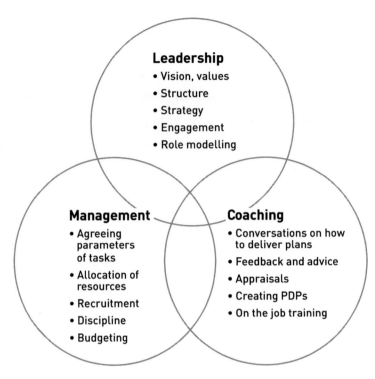

Figure 12: The line manager's role (Downey)

The CIPD Report by Anderson and colleagues, Coaching at the Sharp End, identifies two levels of coaching characteristics: "Primary coaching characteristics comprise: a development orientation; a performance orientation; effective feedback processes; and successful planning and goal-setting activities. Mature coaching characteristics … include: using ideas from team members; powerful questioning; team-based problem-solving and shared decision-making."

It's not an easy option for organisations, however. Cultural barriers and the time constraints faced by managers are cited as the two most common obstacles. The latter, of course, has an element of Catch 22 about it: Why can't you find time to

THE LEADER AS COACH • 137

coach? Because I'm too busy firefighting. Why are you too busy firefighting? Because I don't have time to coach my team so that they can think for themselves. Etc.

Additionally, the organisation that aspires to a coaching culture needs to be wary of setting up people to fail. It needs to ensure that managers are equipped for success through training and supervision and, in particular, additional support is provided to those managers to whom this style does not come naturally.

The Benefits of a Coaching Style of Leadership

A coaching style of leadership is emotionally liberating for the coachee. They typically feel they are more trusted, have more autonomy and are developing personally.

It serves the organisation in that it creates teams that are more reflective and therefore learn quicker, have the capacity to use their own initiative rather than rely on the direction of their line manager, and are resilient – they will keep functioning at a high level when the leader or one or more other team members are absent.

If adopted across an organisation a coaching style of leadership can help achieve a more open and involved culture. This, in turn, supports a move from a hierarchical structure, where the manager is expected to have all the answers, to a flatter more democratic design.

On one occasion I led a business where one of my departmental heads struggled with his temper. Instead of threatening him with dismissal, I made a series of one-to-one coaching appointments with him. Eventually, he booked himself onto an anger management course, which proved to be the starting point for an inspiring story of self-discovery, transforming his relationships at work and at home.

The Limitations of Coaching in the Line

There is, no doubt, a limit to how far one can take coaching your direct reports. It is impossible to ignore the fact that you have a degree of power over the individual and that is likely to colour the discussion to some extent.

Consequently, it is rare that such coaching achieves the depth, level of confidentiality and boundary maintenance that a conversation with an experienced external coach might. Additionally, managers that coach rarely receive the supervision (a one-to-one helping relationship with a qualified specialist) that is the norm for professional coaches, and which serves the function of quality assurance, learning, and restoration.

Finally, as in all other managerial endeavours, the line manager needs to be sensitive to the needs of the individual. Some individuals prefer a more directive style; others may have psychological challenges which warrant a therapeutic rather than a coaching intervention. Some individuals are reflective and grateful for honest feedback; others are resistant to it and may benefit from working with a professional coach.

Key Points

- The leader as coach reflects a move from a command and control approach to a more participative style of management.
- With a coaching style of management individuals typically feel they are more trusted, have more autonomy and are developing personally.
- As in all managerial endeavours, the line manager needs to be sensitive to the needs of the individual. It's not for everyone.

Try This

The next time you review an action plan, concentrate on attentive listening and asking open questions.

Learn More

Stanier, M. (2016). The Coaching Habit: Say Less, Ask More and Change the Way You Lead Forever. Toronto: Box of Crayons Press.

PART 3:
COMPASSION FOR TEAMS

PART 3: COMPASSION FOR TEAMS

PEOPLE, PRODUCT, AND PROFIT

My first job out of university was as a design engineer for a multinational engineering consultancy, one of the leaders in its field. I had a remarkable boss, John Gregory, who was irrationally supportive and forgiving. For my part, I was almost unemployable. Coming from the wrong side of the tracks in Rotherham, Cambridge University had failed to knock off many of my sharp edges—it would take several bosses like John and an exceptionally patient girlfriend come wife to do that.

The attitude of the business and John in particular to profit was interesting. On occasion he would ask "When do you think you could get that finished by?" but he would never demand "I need that finishing today." Most of the time he was more concerned that I was developing the requisite knowledge and skills. Over time I came to realise that it was part of a management style that put people first. In the words of Tom Westgate, a boss that I encountered much later, "Look after the people, they will look after the product and then the profit will look after itself."

In a 2018 interview with Inc, Richard Branson said: "So, my philosophy has always been, if you can put staff first, your customer second and shareholders third, effectively, in the end, the shareholders do well, the customers do better, and you yourself are happy." In other words, look after your staff, and they will look after the customer (and ultimately the shareholders).

Why does putting your people first work so well? You might

think that there is a straightforward answer to this: if you look after your people, equip them to be successful, trust them, and then give them the necessary headroom to perform they will be both capable and motivated.

Whilst this is all true, there is more to it.

And it all concerns mirror neurons – you may recall those from the first chapter of part 1. They cause us to mirror the expressions of the other person at a microscopic level and, in doing so, we feel some of what the other person is feeling.

The contagion of yawning is the work of the mirroring system, and the system also explains why anxiety is contagious and why authenticity is hard to fake—we can often sense in our gut when what someone is thinking is not consistent with what they are saying.

Any leader that puts profit or even the customer first will inevitably engender anxiety in their team. What are this month's figures going to be? What are the latest statistics for customer satisfaction? While these are legitimate interests, if we put them centre stage and worry over them the anxiety will spread.

Even if the rest of the team is unaware of the source of their manager's anxiety, they will experience it nonetheless and it will soak up energy that they could be applying to their job. This will compromise both their ability to undertake their everyday tasks and their capacity to take on new challenges.

If the leader is at ease and concerned first and foremost for her people, those people will have the motivation, the energy and the emotional bandwidth to perform.

And that is why profit is a goal best approached obliquely. It is a dependent variable, and people are the dominant factor on which it depends.

Key Points

- Put your people first, and the product (including customer service) and profit will follow.
- Anxiety about the numbers (or anything actually) is contagious.
- Anxiety in the team uses up energy and reduces their available emotional bandwidth.

Try This

Turn up five minutes early to the next team meeting and spend the time taking a few deep breaths and putting yourself at ease. Observe the impact it has on the mood of the subsequent meeting.

Learn More

Ridderstråle, J. and Nordström, K (2000). Funky Business: Talent Makes Capital Dance. Harlow: Pearson Education Limited.

CREATING A COMPASSIONATE CULTURE

Graham and his wife were brought up in an international Christian movement. In their twenties, with the encouragement of the leadership, they started a church that was a new expression of Christianity. They led the church for seven years, during which it thrived and grew.

Then the head office of the movement arbitrarily transferred them to a more traditional setting. They tried to introduce some of the ideas from their previous posting, but the congregation were set in their ways and opposed them at every turn. After 18 months they resigned from the ministry, retrained and became teachers.

Culture, whilst hard to capture in words, is powerful. Over time people settle into norms of thinking and behaviour which are wired into their brains and may be internalised as part of their identity – becoming 'institutionalised' is actually more common than one might imagine. As Timothy Gallwey points out, once this has happened saying the company is wrong is tantamount to saying "You are wrong."

It's the main reason that many mergers and acquisitions fail to realise their potential. I once worked for a firm of private sector consulting engineers that bought a design office from the public sector. The public sector office was a throwback to a bygone age. The private sector firm seeded it with a number of employees from their existing organisation in the hope of changing the culture. After six months the new intake had lost the will to live, and most of them left.

Radical and sudden changes to culture are difficult to achieve.

If a new market requires such a culture change, then smart companies typically use an internal startup.

Later in my career I worked for a construction multinational that decided to enter the project finance market. Success required investment skills, creative thinking, and initiative. In the market account managers required a high degree of autonomy in order to respond at short notice to changing client needs. It was a world away from the tight control that the traditional construction business required in order to make slender margins on large complex projects.

They solved the problem by setting up an entirely new division with its own premises and with staff recruited externally. The business became the most successful in the market. Other companies that tried to address the market using their existing construction teams failed to achieve any sort of scale.

The following diagram represents some key dimensions of culture.

In developing this I have added another dimension, Candour, to the work of Kets De Vries. Whilst one might argue that Candour follows from Trust, and indeed it is strongly related, I think it is a sufficiently important determinant of individual emotional health and collective organisational success to be identified separately.

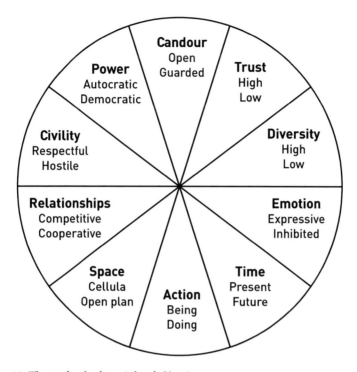

Figure 13: The circle of culture (after de Vries)

We have talked about trust and candour elsewhere within the book. Let's look now at some other dimensions of culture relevant to compassionate leadership.

The Price of Incivility

Porath & Pearson provide an understanding of the price of incivility in their eponymous Harvard Business Review paper. Nearly everyone who experiences unpleasant workplace interactions responds negatively: they may overtly retaliate, decrease their effort or lower the quality of their work. Customers don't have to experience rudeness directly to take their business elsewhere. If they witness an unpleasant interaction between staff, they will draw conclusions about other employees and the organisation.

Through a poll of 800 managers and employees in 17 industries, Porath & Pearson found that when workers had been on the receiving end of incivility:

- 48% intentionally decreased their work effort
- 47% intentionally decreased the time spent at work
- 80% lost work time worrying about the incident
- 25% admitted to taking their frustration out on customers
- 12% said they had left their job because of uncivil treatment.

Incidentally, this research underlines the importance of 'keeping short accounts' – see the chapter on Trust. Episodes of disrespect such as public criticism, exclusion, and bullying lead to unfinished business, which eats into the emotional bandwidth of the individual. If too many episodes remain unresolved, the employee will normally resolve matters unilaterally by quitting.

The Value of Diversity

Most twenty-first century organisations require a diversity of ways of thinking and behaving. For example, an advertising agency needs account executives, who liaise with the client and prepare the creative brief. It's the job of the copywriter and art director to translate that into words and images. Then the production department takes the concept and makes it a reality.

Can you imagine an advertising agency with a narrow window of tolerance, say they only employed creatives? They would ace the copywriter and art director roles, but without the interpersonal skills of the account executive and the execution skills of production, they would be out of business within weeks.

The same thing goes for a computer gaming business. They

require game designers, programmers, and testers. Each of these roles has its own skills profile and list of desirable personal qualities. The company must create an environment in which individuals that embody a wide constellation of skills and traits can flourish.

A diversity of ways of thinking and behaving is normally associated with diversity in terms of age, gender and ethnicity. Less obviously, it is also associated with diversity in terms of personality traits.

For example (and forgive the caricatures), hard-driving accounts executives may also come with a high drive for status and material wealth. They will drive you up the wall with incessant demands for more pay. Creatives may be uber playful and fun-loving to the extent you may find it difficult to spot the time in the day when they are actually working.

It's a key attribute of compassionate leadership to embrace, even love, such diversity. And that means:

- Ensuring that 'outliers', people who may lie at the extreme end of a particular mode of behaviour, are kept safe from ridicule and bullying;
- Explaining the value of diversity to your team, making it clear that it is something you support in principle;
- Recognising the results of unconventional people. "What a weirdo Jon is." "I don't know about that, but his intentions are good, and some of the ideas he brought to that IT project were priceless."
- Recruiting for diversity. This doesn't mean positive discrimination but maintaining a wide window of tolerance when shortlisting candidates.

Finally, there is a symbolic importance to diversity. If we are trying to create an organisation in which the widest range of people find it possible to belong (and not just 'fit in' – see Authenticity and Vulnerability) we need to retain the outliers. Every time one leaves, you are one step closer to a monoculture, where, as I heard someone once summarise it, the attitude is "Fit in or f*** off." He was talking about a business that made losses of the order of £200m per annum and would take five years to turn around.

Power

What we are really asking ourselves here are two questions:

- Do you see your leadership position as a responsibility to serve or as an entitlement to privileged treatment within the organisation?
- Do you view your colleagues as creative, capable and motivated team members, fully capable of doing their job, or as unimaginative minions who have to be told what to do and monitored carefully?

Your answers to these two questions will determine the extent to which power is delegated in your team. Now, you may be saying "surely isn't only the second question relevant to that?" I would argue the two go together: if you see leadership as a ticket to privilege, you will want to keep as much power to yourself as possible.

In the five-year study of 1,435 Fortune 500 companies that underpinned 'Good to Great', Jim Collins concluded that one of the defining characteristics of the outperformers was a leader who combined personal humility with intense professional will.

He termed it 'Level 5 Leadership' and noted "Level 5 leaders channel their ego needs away from themselves and into the larger goal of building a great company. It's not that Level 5 leaders have no ego or self-interest. Indeed they are incredibly ambitious – but their ambition is for the institution, not themselves."

It's a world away from business reality TV shows. In fact, if you like, see this book as an antidote to those shows, which have provided such a naïve and distorted image of what management is like and have done a disservice to business in the process.

It Starts at the Top

Daniel Goleman and his co-authors have noted that "The leader's mood is quite literally contagious, spreading quickly and inexorably throughout the business." The same goes for the leader's behaviour.

An example of this is the hierarchical symbiosis described by Julie Hay. In a business where the board deals with the next tier down on a 'do as I say' basis, it is common to find that the pattern cascades down through the organisation.

Figure 14 represents what is going on in transactional analysis terms – see Transactional Analysis.

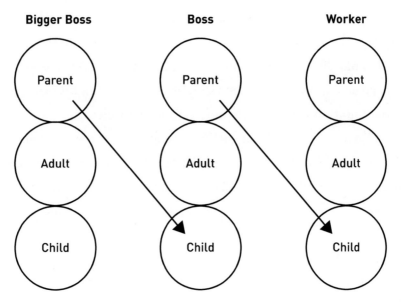

Figure 14: Hierarchical symbiosis (Hay)

It's a less extreme version of the behaviour of the Capo's described by Victor Frankl in his book 'Man's Search for Meaning'. These were concentration camp prisoners who acted as trustees. They beat the ordinary prisoners more cruelly than the SS. Of course, if they didn't comply with what the SS expected of them, they were removed from their position of privilege. But a similar dynamic operates within some organisations.

Therefore, if we want to change the culture of an organisation, we have to start at the top.

We are not just talking about mood and behaviours here. Other things that a leader can do to influence the culture include calibrating reward systems (do the administrative staff participate in the bonus scheme?), setting recruitment criteria (do we pay attention to how respectful people are during the recruitment process?), and determining decision-making methods (what attention is paid to the perspective of the people at the sharp end before decisions are made?)

Now, having said this, if you are not the CEO please don't take it as a licence to hold your head in your hands and do nothing. If all you lead is a small project team, you can still create your own pocket of compassion within a challenging organisational context. The more self-contained your unit is, the easier it will be. And yes, the converse applies sadly.

Key Points
- Culture is powerful and becoming 'institutionalised' is actually more common than one might imagine.
- Civility, power, candour, trust, and diversity are all dimensions of culture that touch significantly on compassionate leadership.
- It starts at the top, but if you aren't the CEO, you can still create your own pocket of compassion within a challenging organisational context.

Try This
Consider where your organisation sits along each of the ten dimensions of culture and take action along one of them in a direction consistent with compassionate leadership.

Learn More
Gallwey, T. (2000). The Inner Game of Work. New York: Random House.

LEADING ORGANISATIONAL CHANGE

This chapter is not about the nuts and bolts of organisational change: governance, the business case, plans, risk, progress monitoring, etc. You can read all about that in your PRINCE2 or APM manual. Instead we are going to focus on how you lead change compassionately, given the emotional impact of change. I have deliberately located it after the chapter on culture because change and culture are inextricably intertwined.

Here we are particularly interested in:

- The intensity of change
- Communication
- Involvement
- Acknowledging loss

The Intensity of Change

The first capacity any senior manager leading change needs to engage is their empathy. You and your directors may be excited by the prospect of change. It's highly likely that the vast majority of your employees will not share your enthusiasm. The outworking of change is something that serves to increase their level of anxiety and reduce their emotional bandwidth.

Even the most robust individuals only have so much emotional bandwidth, and this is why change programmes, like so many other things at work, need to be approached with care and thought. They normally involve both some form of loss and the creation of 'unfinished business.'

I was once coaching the senior management team of a consulting business. They had just been through a management buyout and before they could hold their first board meeting one of the directors died suddenly. The incoming MD had a long list of change projects. I encouraged him to consider how much emotional energy his people had available at that moment.

So many acquisitions start with the board of directors of the acquirer handing down a list of things that are going to change to the management of the acquired company. They are already up to their eyeballs in people who feel the deep loss of their previous identity. There could not be a crasser thing to do than loading them up with the prospect of further change.

So, my first point is, if you can regulate change do so, so that people don't have to contend with multiple change projects at once. I had a divisional MD once who understood this very well. He had one of his team draw up a list of the change projects that head office was imposing. There was 26 of them. He asked his board which we thought were non-negotiable and which we could just pay lip service to. We implemented five.

That might sound like an act of rebellion. I believe it was an act of sanity.

Communication

When change is in the air, people have their antennae up for threats: remember we are more tuned into risk and loss than we are into opportunity and reward – it's the evolutionary adaptation that got us to where we are. Therefore every communication must be considered carefully – content, channel, timing.

Change is always going to provoke more anxiety when a) people don't believe their manager is being straight with them; b) they don't understand the process or the end state or both, or c) they perceive it to be outside their control (see Locus of Control).

So, maintaining trust through authenticity and vulnerability are critical. The manager needs to be a settling influence. Prefer face to face communication over email, as the latter can't capture the expressions, gestures, and tone of voice that will tell people that you are truthful and genuine. In the chapter on Trust, we talked about managing expectations. In times of change, precision is everything. Do not promise anything that you can't deliver and be precise about what you are promising.

If you don't know the answer to a question, admit it. If you yourself are feeling apprehensive about the changes, admit that too while maintaining a positive outlook. If the organisation has been through change before, say a restructuring, and the outcome impacted on the trust of employees, acknowledge it.

Secondly, try to be as comprehensive about what is proposed as possible. If you don't, people will tend to fill in the gaps themselves, and people have a natural disposition to imagine the worse.

For a change programme with a significant impact, consider appointing a transition monitoring team, with a brief to take the temperature of the organisation by inviting comment, soliciting opinion via questionnaires and tapping into the organisation's grapevine. It will provide you with all important feedback on how the programme is perceived and its very existence demonstrates that the organisation is concerned for people's wellbeing. Make sure you publish and act on their findings.

Involvement

Involve your people as early as possible in the change process.

Ideally, they should co-create the solution alongside you. The closer you can get to this the more committed they will be.

Here are some possibilities to consider for generating commitment:

- Workshops help develop a collective understanding of the challenge that the company is proposing to address through the change process.

- Consult people on when and how in the process they would like to be consulted.

- Assemble cross-functional teams to design and inform the change project. Not only will you generate commitment, but you will also generate a higher-quality solution.

- Consult the people affected by the programme. Make the change as real for them as possible by prototyping, user acceptance testing, scenario planning and phased roll-out in order to support their input into the process.

- Recognise that management behaviour is critical, and to be successful, your managers will need facilitation skills and empathy.

Change is the acid test of an organisation's culture. If that culture is sufficiently open, people will be honest about when and how they believe they can add value to the process. If it is sufficiently civil and democratic you will gain insightful contributions when you engage with people. And if the trust is high, people will work with you on the assumption that the company's interest, rather than your persona self-interest, is foremost in your mind.

Acknowledging Loss

Elisabeth Kübler-Ross studied the progression of emotional

states experienced by terminally ill patients after diagnosis. Her model – figure 15 below - is now recognised as applying to almost any experience of loss.

And loss is what we almost always have to deal with in times of change. It may be the identity that people have invested in a brand that is lost after the acquisition; it may be the colleagues that people have lost during a restructuring, it may be a certain way of operating that has been lost in an IT implementation.

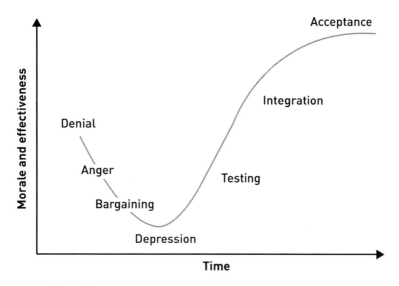

Figure 15: The Kubler-Ross model of individual change

William Bridges urges us to consider who is losing what during a change project. Think of people whose familiar way of being and doing is going to be affected. It may be that the psychological contract between employee and employer is going to change for everyone under new ownership.

Bear in mind that loss is often subjective. However, resist the temptation to argue with a team member's perception of what is going to be lost. Instead, try to understand what is behind their view.

Bridges counsels us to expect 'overreaction' to change. It is the losses that people are reacting to, and it is easy to dismiss a response as 'overreaction' if we ourselves are not being impacted. Overreaction is also typical where previous change projects have not dealt with loss adequately.

As a compassionate leader, you need to acknowledge the losses openly and empathetically and expect and accept signs of grieving. When staff have been made redundant, don't expect the remaining team members to operate at their peak. They will take time. Instead of 'letting them get on with it' and giving your team a wide berth, you need to lean into their grief and create space for people to express and explore their feelings.

I was once involved in an ERP (Enterprise Resource Planning, the software solutions provided by Oracle and SAP among others) implementation. The £180m programme roll-out massively improved data quality and integrity, but the most significant impact of the system was in the way people worked.

People who were used to short-cutting the existing controls in order to make things happen, and managers who were addicted to crisis management, found that their way of working was no longer tenable. The company had to accept the resignations of some staff who, despite training, could not work through the associated anxiety. Sometimes loss can be unbearable.

Key Points

- Maintaining trust through candour, authenticity and vulnerability are critical during a time of change.
- The more you can involve your team, with a genuine intent to benefit from their input, the more commitment you can expect from them.
- Expect to have to handle loss. Acknowledge it, understand it, and expect and accept signs of grieving.

Try This

On your next change project, hold a meeting to brainstorm and discuss who is losing what. How will you acknowledge the losses openly?

Learn More

Bridges, W., & Bridges, S.M. (2017). Managing Transitions: Making the Most of Change (4th ed.). London: Nicholas Brealey Publishing.

EMOTIONAL INTELLIGENCE IN TEAMS

This chapter provides a foundation in team dynamics that we can then build on in the next chapter, which is on Team Development. Firstly, one shouldn't confuse the collective emotional intelligence (EI) of a team with the EI of the individuals that make up the team. Individuals with high EI can use it to play politics within a dysfunctional team.

Most managers don't worry too much about the EI of their team until things start going wrong. They happily concern themselves solely with the items on the left-hand side of figure 16 until one day the wheels fall off.

I was once on a board of directors where the MD's idea of a board meeting was 30 minutes during which he would explain to everyone else what needed to happen. People had given up on dissent, which would generally be met with annoyance or ridicule. And meaningful discussion was a rare occurrence indeed. The first time I heard him own up to a mistake was when things had gone so badly wrong that the company had come within an inch of irrecoverable reputational damage.

Task (content)	Process
Vision and purpose	The emotional climate
Strategy, prioritizing, planning	Communication
Organisational performance	Relationship dynamics
Operational detail	Power, control and authority
Trouble-shooting, problem solving	Rivalries, tensions and conflicts
Action-oriented discussions which produce to do lists	Issues around exclusion/inclusion and feeling valued
Allocation of resources	Issues around difference

Figure 16: The task - process challenge (Bluckert)

It an extreme example of task focus at the cost of process: my MD was attending to the things we needed to, without regard to how we got them done. If he had picked up on the emotional climate (low energy, boredom, and disengagement would be a fair description), he might have thought to ask for the opinions of his colleagues. A little attention to the right-hand side of figure 16 would have improved the quality of the items on the left immeasurably.

We create an emotionally intelligent team by balancing the left and right sides of figure 16 simultaneously; sustaining a task focus while attending to process. In the words of Druskat & Wolff, "It's about bringing emotions deliberately to the surface and understanding how they affect the team's work. Emotional intelligence means exploring, embracing and relying on emotion in work that is, in the end, deeply human."

I know it may sound trite, but the old saying "People want to know how much you care before they care how much you know" has a lot going for it. In a team, people will be so much more motivated to share information and expertise if they feel they are understood.

Building Social Capital

The social capital of a team is the willingness of its members to co-operate, participate and work towards team goals. This, in turn, relies on the underlying commitments of its members; commitments to trust between members, to a feeling of belonging and to the belief that the team members are more effective together than apart.

Such commitments are made real by the behavioural norms of the team. These operate on three levels. At the level of the individual member, the key behaviours are those that improve interpersonal understanding (disclosure and feedback), the willingness to challenge one another and appreciation.

At the team level, team self-awareness is crucial. This is something that is rare in my experience. How often do you reflect on the functionality of the team's behaviours and do you ever ask the rest of the organisation how well they think your team functions? If we seek personal feedback (emotional intelligence 101) then shouldn't we seek feedback as a team also?

Other questions that one might pose at a team level are: Is the team aware of its mood? Does it provide a safe container for releasing emotions? Does it have a can-do attitude? Does it accept responsibility for its decisions as a team or is this where team cohesion ends?

Finally, there's the question of how the team handles its external relationships. How good is its collective understanding of the business environment beyond the boundaries of the team?

Does it build external relationships with purpose? And are its interactions congruent with the values and behaviours to which it aspires?

Team Maturity

In part 1 we noted that the part of the prefrontal cortex responsible for empathy is not fully developed until one's early twenties and therefore we should excuse teenagers some of their more antisocial traits.

In the same way, we need to make allowances for the maturity of a team or lack of it.

It was way back in 1965 that Bruce Tuckman wrote his seminal paper on the developmental sequence of teams. He found that the following pattern is common:

1. Forming – the team is assembled, roles and responsibilities are unclear, the team is heavily reliant on the leader for guidance and direction.
2. Storming – relationships and emotions come to the fore; there may be power struggles, roles and responsibilities are clarified, the leader adopts a coaching style of leadership.
3. Norming – the team adjusts to one another, they come to appreciate individual strengths, norms of behaviour are developed either implicitly, or through discussion, the leader facilitates.
4. Performing – members understand one another, and the team settles down to its most productive phase, the focus is on its goals, but there is a parallel awareness of process, the leader delegates.

The earlier phases may periodically reappear as new members

join the group.

The sequence doesn't have to take forever and an experienced leader, potentially aided and abetted by a team coach, can accelerate the process. However, neither is it instantaneous and therefore to expect a new team to be firing on all four cylinders after a week is unrealistic. Just like the parents of our teenager, we have to make allowances and recognise the pattern of what is happening.

Professor Nigel Nicholson of London Business School observed that the best teams do their work "in a spirit of energized sharing … Individual members seem to know exactly what their distinctive contribution is, but at the same time, they have a feeling of 'losing' their egos in the group. The group takes on a life of its own." That is the standard to which we should aspire.

Key Points
- The collective emotional intelligence of a team is quite different from the sum of the EI of the individuals that make up the team.
- The social capital of a team relies on the underlying commitments of its members; commitments to trust between members, to a feeling of belonging and to the belief that the team members are more effective together than apart.
- Organisations and leaders should understand the developmental sequence of a team as a basis for a) making allowances and b) catalysing movement through the stages.

Try This

Issue a 360-degree questionnaire concerning the performance and behaviours of your team to its internal clients and stakeholders in order to obtain actionable feedback.

Learn More

Druskat, V. & Wolff, S. (2001). Building the Emotional Intelligence of Groups. Harvard Business Review - March 2001.

TEAM DEVELOPMENT

You have just been appointed the leader of a team. It may be a small project team, or you may be the new CEO. But the questions you might ask yourself are very similar.

Orientation

Do we understand our purpose, vision, and goals? – see 'Creating Meaning' below.

How are we going to work together?

How much do we know about each other?

Are our respective roles clear?

Collectively do we have all the skills that the task requires?

Execution

Are our strategy and priorities clear?

Are our processes effective? – see previous chapter.

Do we need to work with internal or external delivery partners?

Monitoring progress

How will we know we are on the right trajectory?

What reports will we prepare?

How can we obtain feedback on our performance as it is perceived by the rest of the organisation?

Communicating

How will we communicate among ourselves?

How are we going to engage with the rest of the organisation and externally?

Team development

How are we going to develop ourselves as a team?

How will we maximise the benefit of the performance feedback we obtain?

What opportunities for debriefing and reflection are we going to build into our work?

Governance

Do we have a clear mandate and accountability?

In the previous chapter on EI in Teams we saw that team EI is not the same as the collective EI of the team members. In the same way team development is not the same as developing the individual members of the team – we cover that in part 4 – but it is about increasing the capacity of the team to achieve collectively.

To the extent that the answers to the above questions are not evident, then I would recommend that they are worked through in a series of facilitated workshops, preferably off-campus, because they provide the platform for team performance.

Creating Meaning

Within the team development agenda, one item deserves particular attention. It is arguable that there is nothing that leaders can do that is more important than creating meaning for their team – writers on leadership as diverse as Kets de Vries, Peterson and Sinek agree on this.

Such meaning operates on two levels; in the societal sense of transcending one's own needs to make the world a better place, and in the personal sense of resonating with the individual's motivational systems – see Motivational Needs and Addiction in part 1.

Peterson writes "Meaning is the Way, the path of life more abundant, the place where you live when you are guided by Love and speaking Truth and when nothing you want … takes any precedence over precisely that."

Most companies serve a useful purpose in society. It is the role of the leader to identify that purpose and to articulate it for their people. Figure 17 below attempts to summarise the huge body of writing that exists on the subject of purpose and its relationship to vision, strategy and behavioural norms.

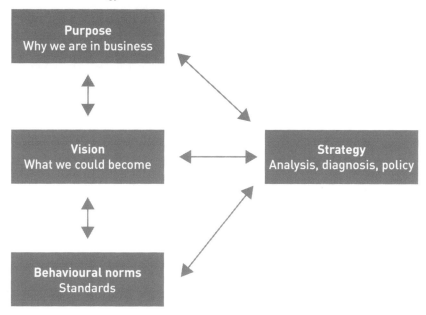

Figure 17: Purpose, vision, strategy and behavioural norms

You might notice that I have used 'behavioural norms' here rather than 'values.' For me, the jury is still out on whether companies can have values. Values are something that individuals hold at the centre of their being and are not amenable to 'cultural conditioning.' One of the corporate values of Enron was 'integrity.' Clearly that was not one of the individual values of its top management.

Of the four areas in figure 17, purpose should come first. You don't need to be the CEO to think about this. Most of us have heard the story of President John F Kennedy's visit to NASA. He saw a janitor mopping up a floor. JFK asked him what his job was and the gentleman said: "I'm helping send a man to the moon." You can create meaning for your team whether you lead a project, manage the office, head up a division or whatever. You might reinforce this sense of giving to society by initiating charitable projects and fundraising within the company.

Concerning personal meaning, the three motivational needs systems, covered in part 1, that are relevant to the world of work are:

1. Aversion – the imperative to respond to threatening situations by antagonism and withdrawal.
2. Attachment – the need for sharing and affirmation, and affiliation to groups.
3. Assertion – the need for play, exploration, and independence.

Some ways in which we can create personal meaning for our team therefore are:

- To underline the headroom available to colleagues to take the initiative in their job (assertion).
- To explain the impact of the individual's actions on the

performance of the team as a whole (assertion).

- To promote individual learning and growth (assertion).
- To promote team working, collaboration and networking (attachment).
- To publicly acknowledge and celebrate achievement (attachment).
- To put in place policies and procedures and to support behaviours that create a sense of individual safety, for example, that address bullying and harassment (aversion).
- To manage the emotional dimensions of change competently – see Managing Organisational Change (aversion).

All this is tempered by one overriding consideration: it has to be authentic and credible. We've already reflected on the fact that evolution has designed us to be able to pick up insincerity instinctively. If our actions then confirm such insincerity, the mistrust and cynicism we release will undo our good work

Remedial Work

The earlier that the work outlined above starts, the less likely it is that intervention will be required later in the day. Team development is ideally a proactive rather than a reactive activity; however, on occasion, you will find yourself leader of an established team that is dysfunctional: trust is low, conflict is high, there are formal grievances in the system, and the rest of the organisation has labelled the team a 'basket case.'

These circumstances normally require the assistance of a professional coach to turn them around and would involve:

1. Confirming or otherwise your perception of the team by running some diagnostics: asking both team members and external stakeholders how they perceive the performance and processes of the team.

2. Gaining a better understanding of the individual team members using Belbin team types (www.belbin.com), for example, and a 360 appraisal.

3. Using a programme such as Kegan & Lahey's 'Immunity to Change' in order to surface hidden commitments and big assumptions.

The outcome of such a process is represented in figure 18. Kegan & Lahey contend that the process should start with individual members of the team diagnosing their individual immunities to change. This helps them get used to the idea of vulnerability and introduces the key concepts on which the team process relies – goals, negative behaviours, competing commitments and big assumptions.

Team improvement goal	Doing/not doing instead (behaviours that work against the goal)	Hidden competing commitments	Big assumptions that sustain the immune system
Create a culture of mutual trust and support	We don't listen very well to each other; we'd rather tell each other We talk behind each other's backs We feel that if we haven't been personally consulted it wasn't a decision We avoid difficult conversations with each other We don't share information We are very judgemental and critical of each other We don't assume the best intent	We are committed to not having to follow anyone else's directions; to our own selfish independence We are committed to winning, even if it means others in the group will lose We are committed to not having to rely on others We are committed to not working through conflicts directly, to not wearing ourselves out We are committed to preserving the pleasure of harshly criticizing and judging each other	There is an inherent conflict between entrepreneurship and collective collaboration – you can't have both We are essentially living in an "every man for himself" world; if things go badly for any one of us, the firm won't be there to back us up If we aren't personally involved in a decision, it can't be a good one Taking our team to the next level is a choice; we don't have to make this step

Figure 18: Typical output from an 'Immunity to Change' process

The big assumptions are typically identified in a two-day off-site workshop. Subsequently, the process calls on the team members to devise a series of experiments to test them. However, the very act of surfacing the assumptions behind the competing commitments raises awareness and sets the stage for change.

No process like this should be implemented without follow up, and so you should commission further feedback and diagnostics after a period of time has elapsed.

Key Points

- Irrespective of whether you are CEO or lead a project team, the questions you should ask yourself are the same.
- There is nothing that leaders can do that is more important than creating meaning for their team.
- Turning around an existing team that is dysfunctional requires effort, emotional intelligence and, ideally, professional help.

Try This

Ask yourself if you can respond positively and with clarity to all of the questions at the beginning of the chapter for your team. Assemble a plan for answering those where you can't.

Learn More

Simon Sinek TED Talk on How Great Leaders Inspire Action: https://www.ted.com/talks/simon_sinek_how_great_leaders_inspire_action

HOW TO RECRUIT LIKE THE DUKE

If you read management books, you will come across numerous formulae for recruitment. For example, Jack Welch, ex CEO of General Electric, advocates the 'acid tests' of integrity, intelligence, and maturity as an initial filter and then his 4E (energy, ability to energize others, edge and execution) 1P (passion) framework.

The Duke Ellington Principle is an approach that I first heard described by Professor Nigel Nicholson of London Business School. It appeals to me as a musician and a coach, and it reflects my experience both as an employee and a recruiter.

Basically, the Duke had two criteria for players in his band:

1. Can you play the music?—technical competence.
2. Do you love the music?—The Duke was seeking people who loved playing jazz in his idiom. Being able to play the music was by no means sufficient for him.

Mirror neurons had not been discovered when Duke Ellington was in his prime, but nonetheless, he obviously appreciated that enthusiasm, like anxiety, is infectious.

If you have a band (or an office) full of people who are clock watching, it is going to be a challenge to raise their performance above the level of mediocre. If you have a band full of people who love what they do, morale is unlikely to be an issue for you.

My first job after university was as a design engineer. It was a job for which I was superbly well qualified academically—first class degree, Archibald Denny Prize for the Theory of Structures, ICE Prize for Outstanding Undergraduate Achievement, senior scholarship—and totally unsuited. I liked design engineering, but I didn't love it. And time dragged.

I actually loved working with people, but it turned out that much of design engineering involved interacting with a calculator and drawing board. For some reason, this had not occurred to me. My employer, a multinational design engineering business, was exceptionally kind. I was a square peg, but they patiently tried me in various diameters of round hole over a period of five years before I resigned to do an MBA.

A couple of years later I had a job as Project Manager for a large construction business. It was a people job, and I loved every minute. And for the following 30 years, I had a blissful working life. I loved the music.

When I became regional director for the office of a project investments business, the Duke Ellington Principle was my go-to for recruitment. The result was an office full of sparky people that broke all the records for performance in our sector. I was quite open about how I approached recruitment, and everyone had heard of The Principle; indeed it was the cornerstone of our business strategy.

So, when you are recruiting, I would recommend that first of all you look for job applicants who can enthuse about the business you are in—that love coding or design engineering or utilities networks or whatever it is that you do.

Check that their knowledge is consistent with what you would expect from an enthusiast. I once had a job applicant who told me (with a straight face) that they felt destined to be a manager. "Oh," I said, with genuine anticipation of an interesting conversation to come, "what was the last management book you read?" "Well, I haven't actually read any books yet" came the reply.

Once you have established they love the music, use work samples and assessment centre tests that will help you objectively determine whether they can play the music—numerical and verbal reasoning, collaborative working, presenting, exercises specific to your line of business.

Objective tests are important because all the research that has been done on interviews has found that interviewers have a bias towards first impressions—they make a decision on the information they receive in the first four minutes or less and then spend the rest of the interview attempting to rationalise their decision. (That's one of many reasons why internal candidates that have a demonstrable track record are often a better option.)

Incidentally, this observation about first impressions is not a character flaw—though I suppose you could see it that way—but an evolutionary adaptation. In former times our survival depended on a split-second judgement of character when we encountered strangers. It's less useful nowadays and particularly unhelpful when we are recruiting.

As a tertiary recruitment matter, you may wish to explore some of the factors that may bear on the resilience of the individual, such as the length of their commute, their interests outside of work – see Personal Resilience.

Finally, don't forget to check you are not hiring a sociopath – see Dealing with Sociopaths.

So, whilst I wouldn't ignore Jack entirely, a multi-dimensional recruitment model has the potential to mask or de-emphasise the things that really matter; the two things that the Duke put centre stage. They helped him create a legendary band. They can help you create a legendary business.

Key Points

- When it comes to recruitment, look for someone with a genuine enthusiasm for what you do – do they love the music?
- Use a battery of relevant tests to objectively assess whether they can play the music.
- Then check for resilience.

Try This

The next time you recruit someone, look for confirmation that they love the music your business plays.

Learn More

Welch, J. (2005). Winning. Harper Collins Publishers.

APPRECIATIVE INQUIRY

I have mixed feelings about appreciative inquiry (AI). On the one hand, there is no doubt that ruminating on gaps, issues, and problems will only serve to reinforce the corresponding neural pathways. Adopting an unremitting deficit-based view is energy sapping. On the other hand, in general, the prospect of loss is a stronger motivator for human beings than is the prospect of reward.

Nonetheless, it is a useful approach to have in one's repertoire, permitting us to reframe a situation and thereby consider it from a different angle. It has the potential to change the engagement and energy when a team is stuck.

The core processes of appreciative inquiry are:

1. **Definition:** Choose the positive as the focus of inquiry – reframe the problem into a desired outcome.
2. **Discovery:** Elicit stories of exceptional performance related to the inquiry topic.
3. **Dream:** A typical AI question would be "Imagine waking up five years into the future and discovering that your organisation has made exceptional performance the norm. Describe to a journalist how your organisation is working."
4. **Design:** What needs to happen to support your vision of the future, in terms of strategy, structure, leadership, decision-making, systems, roles and relationships, products and services, etc?
5. **Destiny:** Identify committed individuals and groups and mandate them to enact the change.

A formal AI process is ideally run by a facilitator trained in the methodology and may take two to three days.

However, one can appreciate how adopting an appreciative inquiry mindset less formally across a team might alter how an issue is perceived and set the scene for a more constructive solution. The invitation to participants to reflect on their positive experiences allows them to voice their unique contribution to the organisation and builds their confidence that they can be part of an inspiring future.

For example, Health & Safety management can often revolve around accident inquiries and the devising of ever more draconian 'preventive measures.' An appreciative enquiry outlook may draw attention instead to the safety culture that is associated with a low or zero accident rate.

AI has also proved helpful for community development, change management, strategic planning, strengthening partnerships, promoting organisational learning and conflict resolution.

So, the next time your sales manager says "This month's figures are looking poor," resist the temptation to ask "So how can we address the problem?" Try instead "When we had that record month last year, what was going right?" AI can be just as well applied to your management philosophy as to the development of your team and organisation.

Key Points

- AI helps us reframe a situation and has the potential to change the engagement and energy when a team is stuck.
- The formal AI process is run by a trained facilitator during a two to three-day workshop.
- However, the manager can adopt AI less formally as part of her management philosophy, when it can often set the scene for a more imaginative solution.

Try This

The next time you are discussing an area of difficulty with a colleague, ask a question like "Cast your mind back to when we did exceptionally well at this. What made things go right?"

Learn More

Stavros, J. and Torres, C. (2018). Conversations Worth Having: Using Appreciative Inquiry to Fuel Productive and Meaningful Engagement. Oakland: Berrett-Koehler Publishers.

FLEXIBLE WORKING

When managers ask me what I think about flexible working, I think of the reply that Andy Dufresne gives Captain Hadley in The Shawshank Redemption when they are discussing tax avoidance, "Do you trust your wife?" except in this case I would ask "Do you trust your employees?" Flexible working is one of those moments when the truth emerges from behind the rhetoric.

Flexible working was led originally by the public sector, then taken up by consulting businesses. It has more recently become a feature of many tech companies. The chart below, taken from the UK Government's Workplace Employment Relations Study, which relates to 750,000 UK workplaces, shows that in 2011 56% of workplaces offered some form of flexible working.

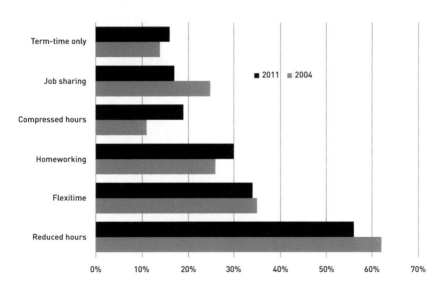

Figure 19: Flexible working trends - from the 2011 WERS

When I say it's a moment of truth, it's homeworking in

particular that I am thinking about, though most of the other modes involve an element of trust, for example when someone is working compressed hours you are trusting the individual to put in the same effort during four 10-hour days that he would apply during five 8-hour days.

Incidentally, when making the argument against homeworking, you might want to consider how well you can monitor the effort someone is making if they are sitting right under your nose in the cube farm. In other words, is not the control you imagine you have over employees in the office illusory?

Many studies have suggested that those who work remotely or who work compressed hours on a voluntary basis, are actually more productive. There are several mechanisms at play here:

- Work intensification can be an act of reciprocation or exchange by the employee: my employer trusts me; therefore, I will honour their trust by working hard. For example, the researchers found that some workers were extending their working day to include the hours they would otherwise spend commuting.

- Flexible working can enable work intensification by removal of workplace distractions – demands of colleagues, social interactions.

- Work intensification can result from the employee being able to expend more effort per hour if they are working a shorter working day or week.

- Work intensification may be imposed involuntarily when a full-time member of staff opts to reduce their hours, but their workload is not reduced accordingly.

Kelliher & Anderson found that remote workers and workers on reduced hours contracts reported significantly higher job satisfaction and organisational commitment. On average, the levels of stress experienced by the workers were lower.

Is it all upside then, for both employer and employee? Well, not necessarily. Most forms of flexible working mean that the employee spends less time in the office during the 'normal' working day. This can have a substantive impact on their ability to work collaboratively and to feel part of a team. Some remote workers have reported a concern that lower visibility might also affect their promotion prospects.

Which takes us back to the start of part 2: Treating One Another as Individuals. A flexible working policy is an expression of trust in your employees and can be expected to benefit both the organisation and the individual, but don't expect everyone to take it up enthusiastically. And if they do, allow them the discretion to modify the arrangement or change their mind altogether in due course as they experience the cons as well as the pros.

Key Points

- In 2011 56% of workplaces offered some form of flexible working.
- Research suggests that flexible working can yield higher productively via several different mechanisms.
- It also improves job satisfaction and organisational commitment and lowers the level of stress.

Try This

The next time you receive a request for flexible working, explore with your HR manager whether a positive response is possible.

Learn More

Kelliher, C. & Anderson, D. (2010). Doing More with Less? Flexible Working Practices and the Intensification of Work. Human Relations 63(1), 83-106.

THE LIFE-GIVING WORKFORCE DESIGN MODEL

I'm not sure why the Life-Giving Workforce Design (LGWD) Model isn't better known. Perhaps it's because the author of the eponymous 2011 paper, Barry J. Halm of the University of Minnesota, died before it was published. Or maybe it is that the paper is written in an academic style that is off-putting to many practicing managers.

Anyhow, I am going to see if I can make it more accessible in this chapter. I believe it pulls together so many themes of the book. See what you think.

The model is based on the study of the regional office ("RO") of a professional services company with 50 offices in 9 countries. During the period July 2004 to June 2007 the office continually improved its metrics for employee engagement, employee retention, client satisfaction, revenue, and operating profit until it topped the rankings for all five indicators.

Halm undertook a post hoc investigation of what had happened at the RO to induce such superior performance. The RO employed 120 professional staff, of which 23 were randomly selected to participate in the interviewing process. The study was directed towards four areas of interest: organisational culture, leadership, employee engagement, and operating systems.

From the initial observations and findings, 22 patterns emerged, which were grouped into seven themes, which were eventually related to the four areas of interest. The outcome is represented in figure 20 on page 195. Halm writes "In this study, the LGWD was constructed by an appreciative culture and was supported by liberating leadership methods and sustainable operating systems that generated employee engagement, resulting in extraordinary changes in performance."

Halm considered the inter-relatedness of the areas of interest central to the success of the model. He contended that it was the synergies between them that led to the exceptional performance of the business.

Let's take a closer look.

Liberating Leadership

Halm describes a pattern of "nurturing management practice" based upon the values of "respect and compassion." There were further patterns of mentoring and coaching and also of participative and democratic principles. The MD articulated a clear vision and expectations and then gave his directors and managers the headroom they needed to deliver on them.

This style was appropriate and successful because the employees were highly experienced, goal oriented and many had worked for the business for some time. One interviewee said "Our MD is really refreshing because he truly gives his directors the freedom to make the right decisions. I can always count on him that whatever decision I make, he will support it, and he will support whatever resources I need to get the job done."

Appreciative Culture

The leadership team was focused on human connection. Interviewees talked about integrity, teamwork and work-life balance. Teamwork was characterised by open communication and whole-team involvement. The flat structure of the business meant that teams could respond rapidly to change in order to meet client needs.

The collaborative energy of the business was supported by camaraderie, employee engagement, appreciation and coaching/facilitating management. One interviewee said "The feeling is not just with me but with all of us. I think one of the reasons our turnover rates are very low is exactly because we value our people."

Authentic Engagement

The recruitment of second careerists was key to meeting the needs of the organisation's clients, namely experience, knowledge and a dedication to professionalism. The organisation followed the Duke Ellington Principle in selecting people who could both play its music and loved the idiom.

The business made a point of valuing the individual through open and frequent communication, something we reflected on at the beginning of part 2. Allied to this was the principle that individuals were assigned to work strategically, that is to projects that were a good fit with their experience, and project leaders were chosen on the basis of the 'best man for the job,' ensuring that power was distributed.

An entrepreneurial spirit in the organisation was enabled by the autonomy granted to the board by the MD, and in turn to employees by the board – an example of a non-hierarchical approach cascading down (see Creating a Compassionate Culture/It Starts at the Top).

This was an organisation that took care of its people in order to take care of its customers – see People, Product, and Profit. The committed workforce created by liberating leadership, an appreciative culture and authentic engagement led to high levels of customer satisfaction. One interviewee said, "The organisation is about procuring the knowledge that is required to go deep into a corporation and become a trusted advisor."

Sustainable Systems

The organisation adopted appreciative methods – see Appreciative Inquiry – which was consistent with the positive atmosphere that prevailed.

The paper notes, without going into much detail, that the formal systems of the business included effective performance management and evaluation, employee recognition and reward and organisational performance monitoring and benchmarking.

The study is a lovely piece of work by Halm, but it does leave one or two questions unanswered, including what events triggered the improvement in performance and was it sustained? Presumably, if the MD were new in 2004, the paper would have said.

Could Halm have intended the paper as the starting point for a larger study? I tried to contact the name given in the paper for future correspondence but received no reply. If anyone from the University of Minnesota can shed light on my questions, please get in touch.

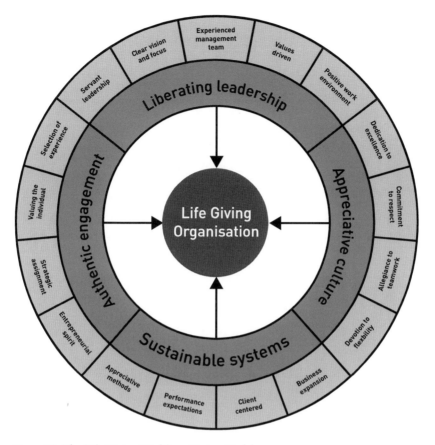

Figure 20: The Life-Giving Workforce Design Model

Key Points

- The model is based on an investigation of the office of a consulting business that delivered exceptional performance over a three-year period.
- There are four main dimensions to the model: Liberating Leadership, Appreciative Culture, Authentic Engagement, and Sustainable Systems.
- The performance of the business was the outcome of the synergies between these four areas: all four acted in concert.

Try This

Share the LGWD model with your team and ask what aspect of it that isn't already part of your practice would be most beneficial to your business.

Learn More

Halm, B. J. (2011). A Workforce Design Model: Providing Energy to Organizations in Transition. International Journal of Training and Development, 15(1), 3-19.

PART 4:
COMPASSION FOR YOURSELF

PART 4: COMPASSION FOR YOURSELF

PERSONAL RESILIENCE

There's a lot of talk about resilience at present and justifiably so. The factors that reduce our emotional bandwidth have become ever more prevalent: a lack of job security, accelerating change, long commutes, litigation, redundancy and so forth.

Resilience is the capacity to overcome a succession of such emotionally challenging obstacles and adapt successfully to changing circumstances. It is strongly related to emotional bandwidth, so if you haven't done so already, I would recommend reading the chapter with that title in part 1 before continuing.

At eighteen, having grown up in Eastwood, Rotherham and attended the local comprehensive school, I washed up on the shores of Trinity College, Cambridge. After I had gotten over the initial culture shock – we didn't have guinea fowl for dinner that often on my council estate - it's fair to say that the following three years taught me a lot about resilience.

Figure 21 presents a model for personal resilience. It introduces four categories of factor that impact on our emotional bandwidth, two negative and two positive.

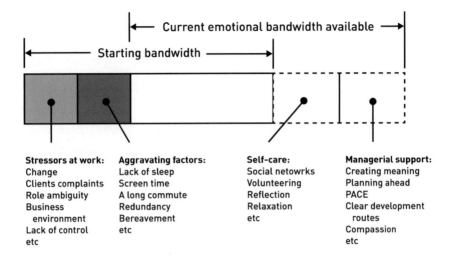

Figure 21: A model for personal resilience

Stressors at Work

These are the adverse or demanding circumstances at work that eat into our coping ability. Prominent among these are role ambiguity, unresolved episodes of bullying and harassment, a feeling of injustice or unfairness, having to wait on the outworking of a change programme.

At one place I worked the Regional Director's job was advertised. One of the applicants was the Commercial Director of the business, a man of exceptional integrity, who had made an energetic and high-quality contribution to the business for more than ten years. Yet, the company chose an unknown outsider, whom they had to fire after six months for falsifying his expenses. In the meantime, the Commercial Director had left to work for another business. A real-life example of the impact of a feeling of injustice.

Another factor is the anxiety in the system we touched on in

Systemic Thinking and again under People, Product and Profit: if the leader of a team is anxious over, say, this month's numbers, soon her whole team will be, irrespective of whether anything has been said.

Aggravating Factors

Not all stressors that eat into one's emotional bandwidth are work-related. Bereavement, a pre-existing mental health condition, attachment difficulties, excessive screen time, debt and addiction are all examples of situations that take up our emotional energy if unresolved.

Self-Care

We have all met people who have 'dysfunctional' ways of coping with stressors and maybe we have experimented with some of these ourselves: numbing, withdrawing or cultivating an attitude of 'couldn't care less.' I have termed these dysfunctional because they are short-term expedients. If we leave them untended for too long, we become less than human – lonely, unable to broker healthy relationships, potentially prone to depression and other illnesses, mental and physical.

Many stressed executives develop a condition called alexithymia, a dead-fish quality. They lose touch with their feelings to the extent that they can't describe their emotions and moods in detail. They have desensitised themselves and/or habitually retroflected (see Defence Mechanisms) over a long period and now struggle to experience fun or react spontaneously. One of the symptoms is an impoverished dream landscape – they can possess such a strong defensive structure that they are unable to recall their dreams.

Self-care involves recruiting the means within our control to free up additional bandwidth.

Social networks such as friendship groups, sports clubs, faith communities, and teams of volunteers all serve to restore our emotional bandwidth by meeting our emotional needs for attention, fun, community, and meaning. Reflection and journaling can help us close out unfinished business and think constructively about relationships.

Transformational learning experiences (see Personal Development) strengthen our cognitive ability and help us process challenging situations more effectively. Relaxation practices, such as meditation and yoga, have both a direct effect and also enable us to 'tune in' to our thoughts and feelings, improving our self-awareness and regulation.

Finally, there may well be some unhelpful mental habits that we need to let go of, for example ruminating on our problems and preconceived ideas of how things "should be," such as perfectionism. Often shifting these will require the assistance of a coach or therapist.

Managerial Support

I provide training on resilience, and on occasion, I have upset my corporate client by taking a systemic viewpoint and pointing out that they could well be responsible for quite a lot of the stress that their employees are under. They don't need resilience training for their employees but compassionate leadership training for their managers.

It's probably not a great business development strategy, though to be fair some companies take the message on board.

In short, if a business habitually practices compassionate leadership – creating meaning, treating people as individuals, listening, closing out unfinished business, using PACE, providing clear development routes, etc (see the rest of this book for details!) - then they will expand the emotional bandwidth available to their employees and therefore the energy available to the business.

Key Points

- Resilience is the capacity to overcome a succession of emotionally challenging obstacles and adapt successfully to changing circumstances.
- This chapter introduces a model of personal resilience that includes four categories of factor that impact on our emotional bandwidth.
- A business can significantly increase the emotional energy available to its employees by adopting compassionate leadership practices.

Try This

Reflect on how you as a leader can increase the emotional bandwidth of your team.

Learn More

Kets de Vries, M. (2006). The Leadership Mystique: Leading Behavior in the Human Enterprise (2nd ed.). Harlow: FT Prentice Hall.

DEALING WITH SOCIOPATHS

Jane, a friend of mine, was an eminent accountant and in love with her job when a new woman, Alison, joined her firm. Alison singled Jane out for friendship and gave her regular gifts.

Then after a while, a rumour started to circulate: Jane had slept with senior members of the business in order to gain her position. Jane suspected Alison for starting the rumour but had no proof. Jane's work in a particular northwest town dried up without explanation. Months later Jane happened across one of her old clients to be informed that Alison had told them that Jane hated travelling to the town and thought it was a dump.

When Jane confronted Alison, she was met with denials and then over time a series of undermining comments.

After several years of this treatment, Jane became an emotional wreck. Tired and disillusioned she left accountancy to start her own business. From time to time she contemplates resuming her old job or taking a different job in the corporate world, but the prospect fills her with dread.

I once worked for someone who was on the narcissistic spectrum. After a honeymoon period during which he was charming and friendly, he made a habit of questioning my version of reality. For example, he frequently claimed that others had said things to him that contradicted my perspective on staff morale.

And then he set about undermining my confidence. On one occasion he subjected me to a two-hour tirade of criticism. I remember asking him at the end of it "Do you not have one single positive thing to say?"

Fortunately, circumstances meant that our relationship ended.

But it was a narrow escape for me. I had begun a descent into depression and anxiety. The parting of our ways came as a huge relief.

Identifying a Sociopath

A word of warning here that more people appear as sociopathic than actually are – see ASPD in the chapter on Personality Disorders - and that an isolated instance of shoddy behaviour does not make a narcissist.

If you can read people well, you have a head start. Once when a new manager joined us, a colleague whom I rated as having emotional intelligence, said to me, "Something is not quite right about …" At the time I suspended judgement, but, sure enough, events bore him out.

Back to mirror neurons. If you have a reasonable amount of empathy, you can intuitively pick up on when someone's feelings and words are not aligned. Normally you will get a feeling in your gut. However, don't expect everyone to share your perspective. Studies have shown that around 60 percent of people tend to follow whoever is leading them, irrespective of whether that leader is malevolent or benign.

Secondly, understand the process and try to spot the signs. If a sociopath is targeting you, you will initially experience them as charming, energetic and fun. If the sociopath is your boss, they may tell you that you have great potential.

Then slowly the climate will change. It will seem that you can't do anything right and that your take on a situation is always wrong. This could well be the start of the gaslighting process. The harder you try to please the sociopath the more displeasure you incur. Their behaviour becomes more and more unpredictable.

Finally, when the sociopath feels the game has lost its attraction, they will behave as if you don't exist. At work, if you haven't become so anxious that you are off sick with stress, they will seek to fire you or demote you.

Taking Action

Now we're going to consider what can be done. The first thing to say is that getting rid of a sociopath will be a challenge. They have remarkable staying power, being prepared to do almost anything to maintain their standing, and their charm hides the dark side of their nature. The situation can be no less dangerous if you are their boss. They may start a whispering campaign against you or accuse you of some form of impropriety.

The key insight is that the sociopath is not going to change for the better. The onus for action is all on you.

Firstly, it is not useful to label anyone a sociopath. You may believe that your colleague has all the attributes and behaviours but using the term 'sociopath' is not going to make life easier for anyone.

Be aware that at some stage they may look to damage your reputation and call into question your work, so keep a record of correspondence and salient events. In the meantime endeavour to do your job to the best of your ability and maintain your reputation among your peers. Take your performance appraisal and its written contents seriously and challenge any inaccuracies.

Ensure you know the content of your company's bullying and harassment policy. A good employer will make it clear what is unacceptable behaviour in the company, and this should include spreading malicious rumours, ridiculing or demeaning someone and making comments about job security.

Finally, be prepared to act. The sociopath will take any attempt to ignore their behaviour as encouragement. Don't confront them: they rarely think badly of themselves, they could become aggressive and they could easily fake feelings of remorse in order to stay in the game.

You have three realistic options: firstly, put as much distance between you as possible, for example obtaining a transfer to another division. Secondly, invoke the bullying and harassment policy and lodge a formal complaint (and be prepared for a fight as the sociopath marshals all the resources at their command to discredit you) and thirdly, simply leave, having secured a new job in advance if possible.

If you are experiencing sociopathic abuse, no action at all is not an option. The legacy of sociopathic abuse can be life-altering. Once you are clear of the sociopath, put it all behind you. You may require therapy to do this. Put your energy and enthusiasm into your new job.

Though awareness of the potential for and consequences of abuse within companies has improved significantly over the past decade, you should assess your situation carefully before making a formal complaint. If you are a manager called to investigate an incident of bullying or harassment, I hope that this chapter has provided you with some insight into the complexities that you may face.

Key Points

- Be aware of the sociopathic process – assessment, manipulation, abandonment.
- If you find yourself working with a sociopath ensure you keep an accurate record of correspondence and events.
- Most of the time, leaving your division or the company will be your best option.

Try This

Familiarise yourself with your company's bullying and harassment policy and brief your team on the same.

Learn More

McGregor, J. & McGregor, T. (2013). The Empathy Trap: Understanding Antisocial Personalities. London: Sheldon Press.

FINDING YOUR VOCATION

Before we come to the section on personal development, which is the "how" bit, if we want to avoid expending a lot of energy wastefully then we need to answer the questions "What do I want to make of myself and what do I have to work with?"

As Jack Welch says in his book 'Winning', "Find the right job, and you'll never work again." Which I have found to be true. When you are doing a job you love it doesn't feel like work. You're fully immersed in a feeling of energised focus, involvement, and enjoyment in the activity, known in psychology as 'flow.'

City of Sheffield Rowing Club used to have a slogan on the wall "Do what you love and love what you do." It's the same idea. But how do you find the 'right job' and how does it tie into your purpose, aptitudes, strengths, desires?

One thing I have found about work – whether you are self-employed or an employee – is that it is difficult to imagine what a job is like until you are actually doing it. Which is a why a certain amount of trial and error, provided you adopt the principle of 'failing fast' is no bad thing: Quentin Crisp said "It's no good running a pig farm badly for 30 years while saying, 'Really, I was meant to be a ballet dancer.' By then, pigs will be your style."

I set out as a design engineer. Though I was eminently well qualified for the job, I was not a fan. There was not enough of a people dimension to it. After an MBA I became an academic for a year. Worse. Even less contact with other people as it turns out. So, I took on a job as a project manager. Bingo. Though it sounds (and is) quite a technical role, it is a job that is first and foremost about collaborating with other people. For the next 30 years, I didn't work.

In my case, the job that I took to wasn't actually one that was aligned with my academic strengths (though one of my strengths is a love of learning, so I picked it up quickly). However, it resonated with my emotional needs for connection with other people and a feeling of achievement.

I am going to digress here briefly. A similar pattern has played out in my private life. I was actually a decent musician at school, playing in my County School's Brass Band and the British Youth Wind Orchestra. But I now realise that it was the social side of music that appealed to me and that I actually enjoyed sport more.

Anyone who has seen me play the many sports that I have participated in – hockey, football, judo (very briefly), rowing, road biking, mountain biking – would be shaking their head at this point. I am not an athlete. But that doesn't matter as far as I am concerned. I love the feeling of movement, of being alive, of team camaraderie, of the great outdoors. So, once again I have (perversely some might say) pursued what I love in favour of what I was quite good at. Blame Mr. Dallinson my games teacher for his irrational encouragement.

I should make it clear that I don't subscribe to the maxim "You can be anything you want if you just try hard enough." Introject that, and it is a formula for a lifetime of disappointment. I think what my life to date has taught me is that you have more options than you imagine – you shouldn't be unduly constrained by your education (or your physique!).

And if you find a job that resonates with who you are - the things that give you life - then a) it feels easy and b) because of the energy and enthusiasm it will release, you will be far more successful at it than in a job you don't enjoy. I don't think I would have been a successful design engineer if I had spent two lifetimes at it, but from project manager I rose to board director of a major contractor and then MD of an SME.

There is a caveat here concerning the raw material you have at the outset. You won't be the next stroke for the Great Britain eight if you are five foot four and 55kg (although if you have a passion for rowing, you might be the next cox.) Similarly, if your drawings skills are so-so, you may struggle as an architect.

To summarise all of this I offer the following model. What gives you life might include autonomy, wealth, collaborating with others, power, order, status, family, aesthetics, adventure, achievement, spirituality, health, sensuality, care for others, meaning.

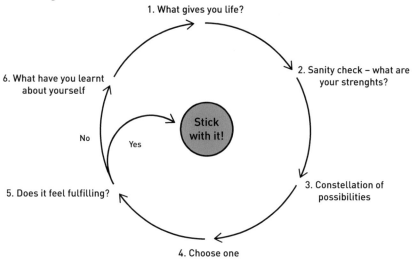

Figure 22: A model for finding your vocation

Let's take an example. If I am looking for autonomy and wealth, and I am good with numbers, an entrepreneur might be an option. However, if I have average energy, it is possible that I might not be up for an 18-hour day until I get the business off the ground. Perhaps I should consider tax consultant or auditor instead?

The next step is to get started. Apply for and hopefully secure a job or an opportunity to shadow someone who does the job. Never mind that it is not what you imagined, does it resonate with you? Does it feel fulfilling? If not, bank the learning and apply for something else, only don't wait years to do it.

Finally, I've always found it helpful to follow the advice of Stephen Covey and write down my personal mission statement during step 1. As you change and grow, you will want to revisit it, but, like journaling, it compels you to focus and reflect on your thinking, in this case regarding your character and your values and principles. The Seven Habits of Highly Effective People by Covey contains a number of examples.

Finding your personal meaning and putting yourself in a position to express who you are in your job is one of the most compassionate things you can do - for yourself and your family.

Key Points

- Before you choose a job, ask yourself what gives you life.
- Your strengths should be a sanity check and not the main criteria.
- Find the right job, and you'll never work again.

Try This

Take time to reflect and write down your personal mission statement.

Learn More

Bolles, R. (2019). What Colour Is Your Parachute 2019: A Practical Manual for Job-Hunters and Career-Changers. New York: Ten Speed Press.

PERSONAL DEVELOPMENT

Personal Development Planning

I know it's tempting to dash straight to that personal development plan form and start typing. Please don't. First, assemble some source material.

If you have read the previous chapter, you may have started thinking about your personal mission. Next you will want to think about your short-term career goals – What skills do you want to acquire? Which role do you aspire to within your current employer? Are you in the right job/industry?

All too many people forget about their long-term goals until it is too late. There will almost certainly be some intellectual heavy lifting required to achieve an ambitious goal. You would like to be head of your department in a large multinational? How are your language skills? Do you have the necessary professional qualifications?

Then you will need a 360-degree appraisal, input from a mentor or coach and maybe some psychometrics.

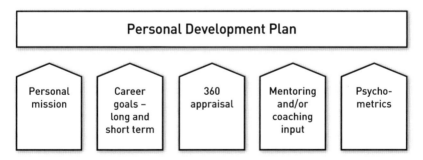

Figure 23: Assembling a personal development plan

Putting together these elements will give you so much more

depth from which to assemble a personal development plan. What? The other people in the office don't seem to be making the same effort? Well, stand out from them and give yourself a head start!

Personal Development Routes

In part 1 we looked at models of human development and reflected on the difference between informational and transformational learning. Whilst you might attend a course to become expert in some aspect of coding, it won't surprise you to know that you can't wake up and decide that today I am going to acquire a self-transforming mind. Yes, it is one of those things that we can only approach obliquely.

My friend, Tony, is from Thrybergh in Rotherham. It's a mining village that used to serve Silverwood Colliery, where my grandfather was a stoker in the engine house. His is not the usual background for a senior management position in a multinational IT company. Yet that's his job. It's one that demands resilience, initiative, and emotional intelligence. How did he develop those qualities?

One of his formative experiences came through The Duke of Edinburgh Award scheme for which he became involved with a Scout group for the visually impaired. When Tony was in his early twenties, the leader died unexpectedly, and Tony took on the leadership of the group. The challenge of organising activities and trips for the Scouts, for example to museums and on one occasion Buckingham Palace, stretched Tony's imagination and interpersonal skills. And spending time with his visually impaired friends expanded his compassion and his window of tolerance.

Most higher order thinkers have got there because they had to change their thinking at some stage or another. And many habitually choose the harder route because they know they will learn more that way. It's called 'leaning in.'

I am going to offer you my own model for personal development – figure 24.

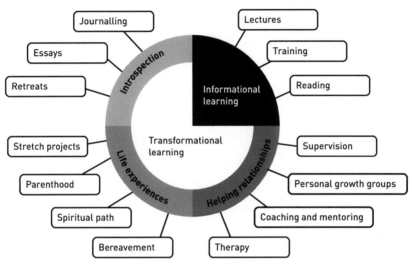

Figure 24: Routes to development

The model has four sectors.

Informational Learning

This is predominantly about the knowledge you possess, rather than about your ability to solve problems. Much of our present education system is dedicated to informational learning. Even where ostensibly you are intended to think for yourself, in say an essay type exam question, the actual answer can be quite formulaic and a matter of you regurgitating the right bullet points in order to obtain the marks.

A good deal of the work you might put into the qualifications for traditional professions such as medicine, engineering, law, accountancy is informational learning. Even modern-day careers such as coding or personal training involve a lot of it.

It's a necessary evil.

Helping Relationships

On the other hand, helping relationships support transformational learning, which is about our ability to solve problems, get on with other people, be creative, take the initiative, leadership. Transformational learning moves us along the path described in the chapter on theories of human development in part 1.

Various approaches will accelerate the transformational learning process and helping relationships is one of them. Incidentally, you may wish to re-read the introduction to the book at this point, as I explain there the distinction between coaching, mentoring, therapy, counselling, and supervision.

A good coach or mentor will help you to deal with greater mental complexity. They will help you examine the way in which you think, look awry at what you had taken for granted, be honest with yourself about your less useful patterns of behaviour.

We're going to return to the mirror neurons we discussed in part 1 in order to think about therapy. People with unresolved stress-inducing memories from their past are likely, on occasion, to communicate the associated feelings to their colleagues. And this, in turn, can cause their colleagues to mirror those feelings, experiencing them as their own. When this happens it can trigger defensive behaviour by all concerned and put a brake on effective communication.

Therefore coming to terms with your own past experiences through therapy can be beneficial for both you and your colleagues. You can expect the emotional freedom it can generate to be valuable in relationships outside of work as well.

Personal growth groups, also known as encounter groups or T-groups (the 'T' stands for 'training') are a form of therapeutic group with the objective of developing a realistic and healthy self-esteem and small group interpersonal skills. It is an experiential learning model in which participants, using a facilitator or trainer, engage each other in a series of conversations over a period of time. This can range from a weekend retreat to regular meetings over many years. The group may initially focus on communicating more effectively and then progress to more substantive issues like trust, as emotional intimacy is established.

In the 50s and 60s, T-groups were commonplace in large organisations, they are less so nowadays. (This may well be because the modern work context inhibits the extent to which many individuals are prepared to make themselves vulnerable.) However, with a little effort, you will be able to find such groups run by therapists, psychologists, and some faith organisations. I have the good fortune to be in a 'book club' organised by a therapist that has been running for five years. Though we started with books, we have broadened out into discussing and debating a wide range of personal and ethical issues.

Life Experiences

These include parenthood (don't do it purely for personal development!), following a spiritual path, bereavement (though you wouldn't deliberately choose that, of course) and stretch projects of one sort and another.

Yoga and meditation are two aspects of spirituality that I have found helpful, as has been engaging with Christianity over a long period of time. More on spirituality in the next chapter.

Stretch projects are about taking you out of your comfort zone, so an assignment at work that is just beyond your current level of ability fits the bill. Some forms of travel can also stretch you, though if you are contemplating a fortnight in Bali at a five-star hotel as a stretch project, save your money and take in a Balinese lodger for a year instead; it will be far more transformative.

I have three daughters who have made stretch projects a way of life. My eldest has run youth projects in some of the toughest areas of Manchester and Sheffield. The middle one is currently working in New York, having studied economics in Spain (in the Spanish language). The youngest seemed to be a quiet soul by contrast, but then when she was 18 casually announced that she was going to study for a degree in the Netherlands and, having spent three years in Utrecht, is now completing her masters in Rotterdam.

They've had to adopt to new customs, rules, and languages and all of this has improved their cognitive flexibility, creativity and empathy.

Introspection

Reflective essays or blogs, journaling, and retreats offer the opportunity for introspection. This requires you to ask:

- What was the challenge I faced?
- How did I feel about it?
- What action did I and others take?

- What alternative courses of action were available?
- Was the solution we arrived at acceptable from a range of perspectives?
- Is it congruent with my values?
- If I faced a similar situation in the future would I do the same?
- What implications does this have for my future practice, plans, work?

In many forms of introspection, you will receive written feedback – obviously private journals are the exception – and this can help counter the tendency to self-delusion that can be associated with unmediated introspection. However, any form of introspection is several thousand times better than thoughtless action day after day.

The Price of Personal Development

We shouldn't imagine that personal development comes free of charge.

Erik De Haan says: "… learning is in the first instance a painful and risky activity. Painful because you have to give something up for it, and risky because it is an excursion into the unknown and you don't know in advance what the situation will be like once you have completed the activity."

During the course of my career, I've learnt to love and embrace the complexity of the human condition, but some of my former independence and convictions have had to be surrendered in return.

A client put matters this way in a bitter-sweet email: "Yes. It's been tough, and it's still ongoing. I made a great leap in recognising that change needed to happen and it's been baby steps with a desire to go back to who I was but, and this is a big but, that person is not there anymore. Meanwhile, as in a shipwreck, the sea keeps crashing in: because life is relentless as always and meanwhile you're trying to build a life raft after deliberately sinking the boat you've been travelling through life on."

In Xanadu

Personal development, of course, is not all about planning. While I was a naïve young undergraduate at Cambridge, working for a Mexborough building contractor in my holidays, a contemporary of mine, William Dalrymple, spotted that for the first time in several hundred years it had become possible to make the land passage from Jerusalem to Shangdu in China. So he applied for a travel scholarship and off he went. You can read about it in his engaging book 'In Xanadu.' Sometimes personal development is about taking opportunities.

I can't resist another anecdote here to illustrate how my 'provincial' perspective differed from that of some of my fellow undergraduates.

In the autumn of 1980, I was walking down Tottenham Court Road in London. A guy in a pinstripe and Crombie was walking on my side of the road in the opposite direction. As we drew level, we recognised each other. He said "Good God, Whitehead! What on earth are you doing here?" I said, "Well, you know, I graduated in engineering, and now I am on a design engineering induction course on Fitzroy Street." He replied horrified "You didn't take engineering seriously, did you? I'm a merchant banker!" It had never struck me that there could be any other career than engineering for an engineering graduate. But hey, I'm not complaining. I found a niche within engineering that was immensely fulfilling, and I don't regret a day of it.

Key Points

- Before you start on your PDP, assemble the necessary background material.
- In the plan itself, aim for a blend of informational and transformational learning.
- If you are serious about transformational development, prepare yourself to feel exposed, stretched and even destabilised at times. Personal development comes with a price, but it's worth paying.

Try This

Identify one aspect of transformational learning that you are not engaging with at present and that would be helpful to you. Incorporate it within your PDP.

Learn More

Arden, P. (2003). It's Not How Good You Are, It's How Good You Want To Be. New York: Phaidon Press.

CREATING PERSONAL MEANING

In the same way that it is difficult to find compassion for others if you can't be compassionate towards yourself, it is difficult to create meaning for others if you can't for yourself.

Creating meaning involves building an understanding of why we value certain behaviours, ideals, and attitudes. This may be rooted in a conventional religion or school of philosophy. Increasingly individuals are drawing from multiple traditions to form their own personal belief system.

I don't have space for the several volumes that a comparative study of such traditions might take, but in any event it would be a futile endeavour: at this point in the book you won't find it difficult to accept that we all set out from vastly different perspectives and experiences of the divine and secular. These will inevitably influence the road we take.

All I can do is commend the task to you.

Personally, I took Christianity as my starting point. Many of the cornerstones of the faith, for example, the Golden Rule "Do unto others as you would have them do unto you," resonated with my personal values.

At the very least, engaging with the one or more major religions gives you an idea of the issues that people have grappled with in the process of creating meaning over thousands of years. For example, most traditional expressions of spirituality include an upward, an inward and an outward dimension. Incidentally, 'spirituality,' at least in the sense that I am using it, simply means relating to the soul or spirit as opposed to physical things.

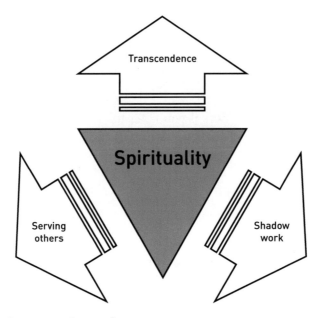

Figure 25: Dimensions of spirituality

Transcendence - the upward dimension - is that experience of wonder and awe at the power of nature, beauty, the interrelatedness of all things, the immensity of the universe.

Serving others – the outward dimension - is the practical outworking of the Golden Rule, or as Dr. Martin Luther King put it "Life's most persistent and urgent question is, 'What are you doing for others?'". This in an area where organised religion has excelled: not only has it been responsible for some of the UK's largest charities, but most faith communities have multiple local initiatives to help the poor and disadvantaged.

Shadow work – the inward dimension - is the process of uncovering those parts of ourselves that we have disowned and rejected. Sometimes, it is an essential precursor to serving others. The best religious institutions provide access to a range of helping relationships, such as accountability partnerships and encounter groups, that can help us here.

The key, in my experience, to the spiritual life is to stay curious. Religious conservatives can get stuck in a literal interpretation of the religious texts, whereas one comes to realise they are a blend of history, poetry, wisdom and an evolving human understanding of the nature of God.

Sometimes it needs a liminal experience – bereavement, serious illness, redundancy – to move us on from a simplistic view of scripture. Then we question the former certainties, and we look afresh at the questions posed by the great religious teachers: What does it mean to die before you die? How do you go about losing your life to find it?

My own experience of this second stage of the spiritual life is that we gain a new respect for others who are at a different stage or are of a different faith (or none) and are working through their own shadow side - our 'window of tolerance' opens up. In my fifties, I took up yoga and meditation as practices that helped me be present in the moment and improved my ability to observe and reflect on my thoughts.

In seeking after meaning, we inevitably face the contradictions, imperfections, and injustices of the world. Humans can be loving, cooperative and creative creatures on the one hand, and at the same time rapacious, ruthless and dominant, particularly from the perspective of all other mammals on our planet. We have a shadow side both individually and collectively.

The key to a fulfilling journey after meaning is to recognise it as just that – a journey - whichever route you choose to take. Whether we uncover meaning through self-help books, discourse or an established philosophy or faith, there is no final destination.

Speaking as an engineer, we approach nirvana or enlightenment asymptotically.

Key Points
- The search for meaning and the experience of transcendence is common to all of us.
- The healthiest expressions of spirituality, whether organised or not, require us to deal with our shadow side.
- One can't develop compassion and find fulfilment in a vacuum. It requires engagement.

Try This
Reflect on MLK's "most persistent and urgent question."

Learn More
Rohr, R. Fr. (2012). Falling Upward. London: SPCK.

YOUR LOCUS OF CONTROL

In mathematics, a locus is "a curve or other figure formed by all the points satisfying a particular equation of the relation between coordinates." It can be a point, a line or a surface.

You might think of your locus of control as the line you draw around the thoughts, behaviours, and situations that are within your control as opposed to those things that are outside of your control.

It's a concept that is tied up with agency: if you recall from part 1, the current consensus is that the unconscious mind is dominant in our decision making. Therefore we often need to surface our unconscious thinking through coaching or therapy before we can make progress. Questioning our locus of control can help us identify when our subconscious is indeed holding us back.

If you have a locus of control that is too tight or confined – sometimes termed an external locus of control – you will tend to believe that you have very little control over your life and attribute your successes and failures to luck or fate. People with a tight locus of control are more likely to experience anxiety because they are continually scanning their environment for the next thing that is going to happen to them.

If you have a locus that is unrealistically wide – sometimes termed an internal locus of control – you will attribute your successes and failures to your own efforts and abilities. People with a wide locus of control are more likely to experience frustration because they tend to overestimate what is genuinely within their control.

Take the 'bad boss' that we discussed in the chapter on Managing Upwards. If your locus of control is too tight, you will believe that your destiny is in his hands and that you have been desperately unlucky to be saddled with such an individual. If your locus is too wide, you will believe that you can alter every aspect of the situation through your conduct: you can either improve your performance to such an extent that you will win him round, you can get to understand him so well that you transform your working relationship, or, failing the first two options, you will be able to influence the organisation to see the error of its ways and move him out.

If your locus is 'healthy', then you may see that the situation is not completely out of your hands, that the first two options are viable and may or may not work out, but that influencing the organisation so that it moves him on is magical thinking. Therefore if the first two fail and you really can't tolerate working with him, patience or your departure are the only two realistic options.

However, from this simple example, we can still see that a disposition towards an unrealistically wide locus is normally better than a locus that is too tight: you may waste some time and energy trying to influence matters to no avail, but this is preferable to feeling completely powerless in a challenging situation.

In my first job, I had a colleague, who like me was in his twenties, and who sat on the next desk. He spent a good proportion of his day bemoaning his situation and how joyless his role was. I lost touch with him after I had left but years later found myself sheltering from torrential rain under a shop canopy in Sheffield city centre. I looked to my side, and there he was. "Jonathan," I said, "How are you doing?" "Well, you know, Chris," he said "It's golden handcuffs now. I'm just waiting to draw my pension." He had spent forty years watching the clock in a job that was a misery to him. That is an external locus of control in operation.

Often a tight or external locus of control is due to an attitude that you have introjected or swallowed whole, often from your parents – see Defence Mechanisms. In South Yorkshire where I come from a common one was "You have a family to support so, irrespective of what your job holds, you need to knuckle down and get on with it."

My father-in-law, Frank Quail, was born into a mining family and when his father died, despite showing promise at school, he was sent by his mother to work down the pit to provide for them. In his late twenties, he married Renee, a wage clerk at the pit. He had become resigned to his lot, but his wife was not. She pushed him to take a job as a riveter, for half his pit wage, and then, when a vacancy arose, as a fireman. It meant a further drop in wages, but a better quality of life for the two of them.

The fire brigade job meant that Frank had the time and energy to enjoy ballroom dancing – he and Renee were in Connie Grant's formation dancing team and danced at venues across Europe – and when the children arrived, to enjoy time off caravanning.

It's interesting how themes replay themselves down the generations – we reflected on this a little in part 1 – and when I married Frank's daughter Judi I might have been prepared to put up with being unhappy at work myself. However, she had her mother's outlook and wouldn't allow me to settle for second best.

Key Points

- Your locus of control is the mental boundary you might draw around the things that are within your control.
- People with an internal locus of control tend to assume that their successes and failures are down to their own efforts and abilities, whereas people with an external locus put it down to luck and fate. Neither is correct!
- Questioning our locus of control can help us identify when our subconscious is indeed holding us back from taking the initiative.

Try This

Choose a situation where you feel stuck right now. Ask yourself if your beliefs about your locus of control in that situation are correct. Maybe ask a friend for their opinion.

Learn More

Shapiro, D., Schwarz, C. & Astin, J. (1996). Controlling Ourselves, Controlling Our World: Psychology's Role in Understanding Positive and Negative Consequences of Seeking and Gaining Control. American Psychologist. December 1996. p1213-1230.

CONCLUSION

I hope this book has piqued a curiosity in you about why people think like they do. More than that I hope that it has widened your 'window of tolerance.' In the final analysis, we are all broken and imperfect and could benefit from more compassion for ourselves and for others.

Below I have provided a map of the terrain we have covered. I have grandly entitled it a compassionate leadership meta model.

We set out by considering just what is doing our thinking. We looked at how the human brain has evolved into an organ that is both remarkably sophisticated and incredibly fragile. We found out that our neural networks take in all of our major organs as well as our brain and that we are also (imperfect) receiving stations for the thoughts and feelings of others.

We went on to look at how we think, what is behind our uniqueness and that of others. It became apparent that when others communicate with us, they are doing so from a perspective that is coloured by their past experiences, particularly those of early childhood, and their genetics. And the majority of their thinking is unconscious. Oh, and we are doing the same!

Then it was time to apply some of our foundational learning. We took in what makes attentive listening so special, why authenticity can't be faked, and the importance (and complexity) of trust. We considered the relevance of the therapeutic approaches of Carl Rogers and Dan Hughes to leadership and thought about some of the issues involved in managing performance.

We extended the conversation to working with teams. How can we create a compassionate culture? What is the emotional intelligence of a team? What can Duke Ellington teach us about recruitment? We looked at how appreciative enquiry can help us look at an issue from a fresh perspective.

Finally, we completed this arc of learning with caring for yourself, without which none of the rest can happen. We touched on personal resilience, handling sociopaths, finding your vocation and your locus of control. We discovered that personal development is less about informational learning and more about transformational learning, and took in some of the associated pathways.

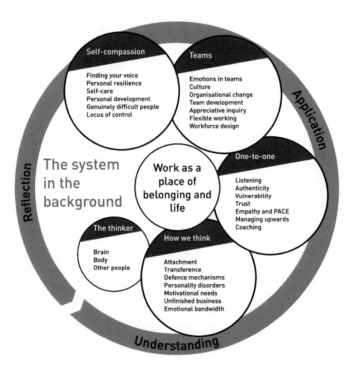

Figure 26: A Compassionate leadership Meta Model

Some Further Suggestions for Leading with Compassion

I hope it's apparent by now that compassionate leadership is not just about thoughts and feelings, but about actions. I've made some suggestions for action in the 'Try This' bullet points within parts 2-4. Here are some more.

- So far as possible, be whom you truly and authentically are. (see Authenticity and Vulnerability)
- Listen attentively to your colleagues without thought of interruption and observe the positive impact that it has on the quality of their thinking. (see Treating One Another as Individuals)
- When someone brings you a problem, try asking "Can you tell me about when we did this really well?" (see Appreciative Inquiry)
- Take every opportunity to appreciate your colleagues and be thankful for the contribution they make (see The Life-Giving Workforce Design Model).
- Look out for the 'outliers' in your organisation. Go out of your way to connect with them (see Creating a Compassionate Culture).
- Treat all allegations of bullying and harassment seriously (see Team Development).
- When difficult situations arise, centre yourself and adopt PACE (see PACE).
- Recruit people who love the music. (How to Recruit Like the Duke).
- Create societal and personal meaning for your team (see Team Development).

Some Suggestions for Self-Care

And remember, unless you take care of yourself you won't be able to care for others.

- Get plenty of sleep (see Personal Resilience).
- Maintain your social network (ibid).
- Meditate (ibid).
- Maybe explore a spiritual path (ibid).
- Keep a daily journal (ibid).
- Find a job you love (see Finding Your Vocation).
- Take your personal development seriously (see Personal Development).
- Differentiate between the things you can and can't control (see Your Locus of Control).
- Close out your unfinished business either with the person involved or a therapist (ibid).
- Make the most of the opportunities that come your way (see Personal Development).

I hope that you enjoy the journey and that what you have read here will help make it richer and rewarding. And I hope you have the delight of helping to create a 'place of belonging.' A more purposeful and satisfying work life is out there — *Carpe diem.*

FOOD FOR THOUGHT

A leader is best
When people barely know he exists,
Not so good when people obey and acclaim him,
Worst when they despise him…
But of a good leader, who talks little,
When his work is done, his aim fulfilled,
They will all say, "We did this ourselves."
Lao-tse

When you talk, you are only repeating what you already know,
but if you listen, you may learn something new.
Dalai Lama

The secret of a successful career is to make sure that the people
around you are learning and developing and feeling good about
what they do.
Dr. Ray Jones

The most revered bosses view their leadership as a service to the
people, a custodianship within the firm's life span. What matters
is that the gene pool he leaves is stronger than when he arrived,
not that he accumulated personal riches or was famous for a day
or two.
Nigel Nicolson

Too many laws, too few examples.
St. Just

I am not impressed by your position, title, and money. I am impressed by how you treat others.

Unknown

REFERENCES

Foreword

I think Andy Cope nails it when he uses the term 'Pop-Up Leadership'…

Cope, A., Martin, M. and Peach, J. (2018) Leadership: The Multiplier Effect. London: Hodder & Stoughton. p35

Introduction

Gareth Morgan has used the terms 'instrument of domination' and 'psychic prison' to describe some workplaces.

Morgan, G. (1997). Images of Organisation. California: Sage.

It's a viewpoint that Ed and Tom have in common with leaders of some of the world's most successful multinationals, including Richard Branson, Herb Kelleher, and Tim Cook.

Branson, R. (2006). Screw It, Let's Do It: Lessons in Life. London: Virgin Books.

Freiburg, K. & Freiburg, K. (2001). Nuts!: Southwest Airlines' Crazy Recipe for Business and Personal Success. New York: Texere.

Kahney, L. (2019). Tim Cook: The Genius Who Took Apple to the Next Level. New York: Penguin.

Daniel Siegel describes as "the band of arousal (of any kind) within which an individual can function well."

Siegel, Daniel J. (2011). Mindsight: The New Science of Personal Transformation, New York: Bantam. p137

The Brain
It is what Steve Peters calls our 'chimp brain.'

Peters, S. (2012). The Chimp Paradox: The Mind Management Programme Programme for Confidence, Success, and Happiness. London: Vermilion.

the part of the prefrontal cortex responsible for empathy is not fully developed until one's early twenties

Hughes, D. & Baylin, J. (2012), Brain-Based Parenting: The Neuroscience of Caregiving for Healthy Attachment. London: Norton. p42

Daniel Siegel describes mirror neurons as the "root of empathy."

Siegel, Daniel J. (2011). Mindsight: The New Science of Personal Transformation, New York: Bantam. p60

The Mind and Body
Siegel defines it as "a relational and embodied process that regulates the flow of energy and information."

Siegel, Daniel J. (2011). Mindsight: The New Science of Personal Transformation, New York: Bantam. p52

The model in figure 2 above brings the mind and body together

Bachkirova, T. (2011). Developmental Coaching: Working with the Self. Maidenhead: McGraw-Hill/Open University Press.

Human Agency
Bachkirova contends "… decisions are being made, not by a conscious rational agent, but by the underlying [unconscious] processes."

Bachkirova, T. (2011). Developmental Coaching: Working with the Self. Maidenhead: McGraw-Hill/Open University Press. p41

Attachment
NICE estimate that 30 to 35% of children in the UK have an insecure attachment.

NICE (2015). Clinical Guideline NG26. Children's Attachment: Attachment in Children and Young People who are Adopted from Care, in Care or at High Risk of Going into Care. Consultation Draft May 2015.

Around 10% of the general population but 80% of high-risk infants, such as the children of drug-addicted parents, have this style.

Ibid

A brilliant account can be found in Brain-Based Parenting by Dan Hughes and Jonathan Baylin.

Hughes, D. & Baylin, J. (2012), Brain-Based Parenting: The Neuroscience of Caregiving for Healthy Attachment. London: Norton.

Projection

As Grant & Crawley point out, "the concept of projection has been part of human understanding at least since Biblical times…

Grant, J. & Crawley. J (2002), Transference and Projection: Mirrors to the Self. Maidenhead: Open University. p20

Defence Mechanisms

Here are some common ones.

Palmer, S. & Whybrow, A. (2007). Handbook of Coaching Psychology: A Guide for Practitioners. London: Routledge. p141

Personality Disorders

According to the Mental Health Foundation…

Mental Health Foundation. (2016). Fundamental Facts about Mental Health 2016. London: Mental Health Foundation.

Researchers Babiak & Hare estimate that 1 percent of the

population are psychopaths

Babiak, P. & Hare, R. (2007). Snakes in Suits: When Psychopaths go to Work. New York: Harper. p18

By way of comparison, some 5% of the population have ASPD and around 50% of the prison population.

McGregor, J. & McGregor, T. (2013). The Empathy Trap: Understanding Antisocial Personalities. London: Sheldon Press. p2

Sociopaths have a knack of identifying suitable apaths.

Ibid p38

Unfinished Business and Emotional Bandwidth
As coach Peter Bluckert observes "Some teams are sinking under the weight of their historic unfinished business."

Bluckert, P. (2015). Gestalt Coaching: Right Here Right Now. New York: McGraw-Hill. p12

Transactional Analysis
Berne expressed the view that the psychological dimension of such transactions is normally dominant

Berne, E. (1964). Games People Play: The Psychology of Human Relationships. London: Penguin Random House.

Transactional analysis can help us understand why this formula for handling customer-complaints can be so effective

McFarlan, W. (2003). Drop the Pink Elephant: 15 Ways to Say What You Mean and Mean What You Say. Chichester: Capstone. p155

Motivational Needs and Addiction
The human being has five basic motivational needs systems

Lichtenberg, J. (1989). Psychoanalysis and Motivation. London: The Analytic Press.

...and has been reported in relation to cocaine, amphetamine, morphine, and nicotine...

Steketee, J. and Kalivas, P. (2011). Drug Wanting: Behavioral Sensitization and Relapse to Drug-Seeking Behavior. Pharmacological Review 2011 June; 63(2): 348–365.

Alcoholics Anonymous describes the psychological cycle of addiction as...

Brand, R. (2017). Recovery: Freedom from Our Addictions. London: Bluebird.

Berne contends that numbing is only part of the story.

Berne, E. (1964). Games People Play: The Psychology of Human

Relationships. London: Penguin Random House. p64 et seq

Nir Eyal explains that successful apps depend on…

Eyal, N. (2014). Hooked: How to Form Habit Building Products. New York: Penguin.

Theories of Human Development
Let's follow the advice of Stephen Covey and "begin with the end in mind."

Covey, S. (1999). The 7 Habits of Highly Effective People: Restoring the Character Ethic. London: Simon and Schuster.

Bachkirova draws on the work of other psychologists and academics to identify a progression in our cognitive (thinking) style…

Bachkirova, T. (2011). Developmental Coaching: Working with the Self. Maidenhead: McGraw-Hill/Open University Press. p49

In this table, the cognitive style stages are drawn from the work of Kegan & Lahey…

Kegan, R. & Lahey, L. (2009). Immunity to Change: How to Overcome it and Unlock the Potential in Yourself and Your Organisation. Boston: Harvard Business Review Press. p52

Treating One Another As Individuals

Nancy Kline observes that "The quality of a person's attention determines the quality of other people's thinking."

Kline, N. (1999). Time to Think: Listening to Ignite the Human Mind. London: Ward Lock. p17

Carl Rogers said: "I have come to trust the capacity of persons to explore...

Rogers, C. (1980). A Way of Being. New York: Mariner. p38

Authenticity and Vulnerability

Her books Rising Strong, The Gifts of Imperfection and Dare to Lead are all classics in the field.

Brown, B. (2017). Dare to Lead. London: Vermilion.

Brown, B. (2015). Rising Strong. London: Vermilion.

Brown, B. (2010). The Gifts of Imperfection. Minnesota: Hazelden.

Brene Brown writes...

Brown, B. (2010). The Gifts of Imperfection. Minnesota: Hazelden. p126

Ray Dalio …contends …

Dalio, R. (2017). Principles. New York: Simon and Schuster.

I was reading Peter Bluckert's book, Gestalt Coaching

Bluckert, P. (2015). Gestalt Coaching: Right Here Right Now. New York: McGraw-Hill. p113

Trust
I like Charles Feltman's, which ties in with the previous chapter: "Trust is…

Feltman, C. (2009). The Thin Book of Trust. Oregon: Thin Book Publishing Company. p7

As Ridderstråle and Nordström observe…

Ridderstråle, J. and Nordström, K (2000). Funky Business: Talent Makes Capital Dance. Harlow: Pearson Education Limited.

Managing Upwards
Williams & Miller identified five distinct categories of executive and five associated ways of influencing.

Williams, G. & Miller R. (2002). Change the Way You Persuade. Harvard Business School Publishing Corporation.

Managing Individual Performance
…what Ronald Heifetz calls 'technical' versus 'adaptive' challenges

Heifetz, R. (1998). Walking the Fine Line of Leadership. The Journal for Quality and Participation, 21(1), 8-14.

The Manager as Coach
Building on the work of Myles Downey…

Downey, M. (2003). Effective Coaching: Lessons from the Coach's Coach. Ohio: Thompson. p97

The CIPD Report by Anderson and colleagues, Coaching at the Sharp End…

Anderson, V., Rayner, A. & Schyns, B. (2009). Coaching at the Sharp End: The Role of Line Managers in Coaching at Work. CIPD.

Creating a Compassionate Culture
As Timothy Gallwey points out, once this has happened saying the company is wrong is tantamount to saying "You are wrong."

Gallwey, T. (2000). The Inner Game of Work. New York: Random House. p20

In developing this I have added another dimension, Candour, to the work of Kets De Vries

Kets de Vries, M. (2006). The Leadership Mystique: Leading Behavior in the Human Enterprise (2nd ed.). Harlow: FT Prentice Hall. p177

Porath & Pearson provide an understanding of the price of incivility...

Porath, C. & Pearson, C. (2013). The Price of Incivility. Harvard Business Review January – February 2013.

In the five-year study of 1,435 Fortune 500 companies that underpinned 'Good to Great', Jim Collins...

Collins, J. (2010). Good to Great. London: Random House. p21

Daniel Goleman and his co-authors note that...

Goleman, D., Boyatzis, R. & McKee, A. (2013) Primal Leadership: Unleashing the Power of Emotional Intelligence. Boston: Harvard Business Review Press. p44

An example of this is the hierarchical symbiosis described by Julie Hay

Hay, J. (2009). Transactional Analysis for Trainers. Hertford: Sherwood Publishing. p84

It's a less extreme version of the behaviour of the Capo's described by Victor Frankl in his book Man's Search for Meaning

Frankl, V. E. (1959). Man's Search for Meaning. London: Random House.

Leading Organisational Change
I alluded to the work of Elisabeth Kübler-Ross...

Wilson, Carol. (2008). Tools of the Trade: Elisabeth Kubler Ross' Change Curve Five-stage Model. Training Journal, March 2008, 56-57.

William Bridges urges us to consider who is losing what during a change project.

Bridges, W., & Bridges, S.M. (2017). Managing Transitions: Making the Most of Change (4th ed.). London: Nicholas Brealey Publishing.

Emotional Intelligence in Teams
In the words of Druskat & Wolff, "It's about bringing emotions deliberately to the surface...

Druskat, V. & Wolff, S. (2001). Building the Emotional Intelligence of Groups. Harvard Business Review - March 2001.

It was way back in 1965 that Bruce Tuckman wrote his seminal paper...

Tuckman, B. (1965). Developmental Sequence in Small Groups. Psychological Bulletin, 63(6), pp 384-399.

Professor Nigel Nicholson observed that the best teams do their work "in a spirit of energized sharing...

Nicholson, N. (2000). Managing the Human Animal. London: Texere. p56

Team Development

...writers on leadership as diverse as Kets de Vries, Peterson and Sinek agree on this.

Kets de Vries, M. (2006). The Leadership Mystique: Leading Behavior in the Human Enterprise (2nd ed.). Harlow: FT Prentice Hall. p253

Peterson, J. (2018). 12 Rules for Life. London: Allen Lane. Chapter 7

Sinek, S. (2009). Start with Why: How Great Leaders Inspire Everyone to Take Action. London: Penguin.

Using a programme such as Kegan & Lahey's 'Immunity to Change'...

Kegan, R. & Lahey, L. (2009). Immunity to Change: How to Overcome it and Unlock the Potential in Yourself and Your Organisation. Boston: Harvard Business Review Press.

The Duke Ellington Principle

For example, Jack Welch, ex CEO of General Electric...

Welch, J. (2005). Winning. Harper Collins Publishers.

Flexible Working
...taken from the UK Government's Workplace Employment Relations Study...

Department for Business, Innovation, and Skills. The 2011 Workplace Employment Relations Study.

Many studies have suggested that those who work remotely or who work compressed hours on a voluntary basis are actually more productive.

Kelliher, C. & Anderson, D. (2010). Doing More with Less? Flexible Working Practices and the Intensification of Work. Human Relations 63(1), 83-106.

Kelliher & Anderson found that...

Ibid

The Life-Giving Workforce Design Model
Perhaps it's because the author of the eponymous 2011 paper...

Halm, B. J. (2011). A Workforce Design Model: Providing Energy to Organizations in Transition. International Journal of Training and Development, 15(1), 3-19.

Dealing with Sociopaths

Read Snakes in Suits by Babiak & Hare and/or The Empathy Trap by McGregor & McGregor.

Babiak, P. & Hare, R. (2007). Snakes in Suits: When Psychopaths go to Work. New York: Harper.

McGregor, J. and McGregor, T. (2013). The Empathy Trap: Understanding Antisocial Personalities. London: Sheldon Press.

Finding Your Vocation

As Jack Welch says in his book Winning...

Welch, J. (2005). Winning. Harper Collins Publishers. p255

...I've always found it helpful to follow the advice of Stephen Covey and write down my personal mission statement at step 1.

Covey, S. (1999). The 7 Habits of Highly Effective People: Restoring the Character Ethic. London: Simon and Schuster.

Personal Development Planning

Erik De Haan (2008 p24) says...

De Haan, E. (2008). Relational Coaching: Journeys towards Mastering One-to-One Learning. Chichester: Wiley. p24

You can read about it in his engaging book 'In Xanadu.'

Dalyrymple, W. (1989). In Xanadu: A Quest. London: Collins.

Creating Personal Meaning

...the questions posed by the great religious teachers: What does it mean to die before you die? How do you go about losing your life to find it?

Bourgeault, C. (2008). The Wisdom Jesus: Transforming Heart and Mind - A New Perspective on Christ and His Message. Shambhala, 23-24.

INDEX

'bad' bosses, 124
acceptance, 114
acknowledging loss, 160
adaptive challenges, 33, 131, 132, 250
ADD, 53
addiction, 61, 62, 173
ADHD, 53
adrenal glands, 13
adult mental development, 74
agency, 3, 25, 26, 27, 85, 150, 231
agoraphobia, 52
Alcoholics Anonymous, 63, 246
alcoholism, 63
alexithymia, 16, 201
amgydala, 30
amygdala, 12, 13, 15
anterior cingulate cortex, 31
anti-social personality disorder, 50, 53, 54, 206, 245
anxiety, contagious nature of, 144
apath, 55
appraisals, 131
appreciative inquiry, 183, 185, 194, 237
arousal, states of, 12
attachment, 29, 30, 31, 32, 33, 58, 175, 201
attachment, insecure-ambivalent, 30
attachment, insecure-avoidant, 30
attachment, secure, 30
attentive listening, 91
authenticity, 2, 17, 95, 96, 97, 98, 123, 144, 152, 159, 163, 175, 237, 248
autonomic nervous system, 19
Bachkirova, Tatiana, 23, 26, 74, 243, 247
bereavement, 52, 120, 201, 221, 229
Berne, Eric, 63, 67, 246
bipolar disorder, 51
blogging, 222
Bluckert, Peter, 59, 97, 245, 249
book club, 221
brain, left side, 15
brain, mammalian, 12
brain, new mammalian, 14
brain, reptilian, 12
brain, reward system, 32, 62
brain, right side, 15

Branson, Richard, 5, 143, 241
Bridgewater, 97, 98
Brown, Brene, 95
bullying, 54, 57, 84, 113, 150, 151, 175, 200, 207, 208, 237
change programme, 58, 84, 159, 200
change, organisational, 157
character, development of, 74
check in, the, 91
coaching, 2, 6, 17, 27, 35, 36, 37, 41, 57, 73, 129, 130, 132, 135, 136, 137, 138, 139, 157, 168, 192, 193, 220, 231, 262
cognitive style, 74, 247
conflict, 70, 72
confluence, 45
congruence, 96, 107, 108, 109, 110, 111, 168, 223
conscious mind, 20, 26
Cook, Tim, 5, 241
corpus callosum, 15
cortisol, 13, 16
counselling, 6, 29, 121, 220
Covey, Stephen, 73, 214, 247, 255
creating meaning for a team, 172
creating personal meaning, 227, 256
Crisp, Quentin, 211
culture, 4, 25, 81, 82, 91, 92, 110, 132, 137, 147, 148, 149, 154, 155, 157, 160, 184, 191, 199
curiosity, 115, 117, 120
Dalio, Ray, 97, 249
Dalrymple, William, 224
defence mechanism, 39, 40, 42, 44, 47
defence mechanisms, 43, 63, 201, 233
deflection, 44
depression, 16, 50, 51, 55, 120, 125, 201, 206
desensitisation, 44
developmental domains, 76
developmental stages, 22
diversity, 5, 7, 90, 150, 151, 152, 155
dopamine, 32, 62, 63
dreams, 201
Duke Ellington Principle, 5, 179, 180, 193, 237, 253
ego, 21, 22, 39, 63, 67, 68, 69, 70, 71, 72, 74, 84, 125, 153
ego state, 63, 67, 68, 69, 70, 72, 125
emotional bandwidth, 43, 57, 91, 144, 145, 150, 157, 199, 201, 202,

203, 245
emotional intelligence in teams, 165
emotional pain, 17
empathy, 14, 17, 45, 53, 54, 55, 107, 111, 113, 115, 117, 120, 157, 160, 168, 206, 222, 242
encounter groups, 221, 229
entropy, 81
feedback, 39, 42, 43, 44, 109, 110, 111, 132, 136, 138, 159, 167, 170, 171, 172, 177, 223
Feltman, Charles, 99, 249
finding your vocation, 211, 238, 255
flexible working, 187, 190, 254
flow, 15, 20, 23, 62, 83, 119, 211, 242
foster parents, 29
Freud, Sigmund, 3, 20, 35
frontal cortex, 14
gaslighting, 54, 206
General Practitioners, 79, 80
generalised anxiety disorder, 51
Golden Rule, 227, 228
Goodall, Harvey, 90
Gregory, John, 1, 143
groupthink, 45
gut instinct, 19
Halm, Barry, 191, 192, 194, 196, 254
harassment, 57, 84, 175, 200, 207, 208, 237
helping relationships, 220
hippocampus, 12, 13, 15, 16
homeostasis, 81
Hughes, Dan, 4, 31, 33, 113, 115, 242, 244
hypothalamus, 12, 13
incivility, 149, 150, 251
influencing, 20, 123, 126, 127, 232, 249
informational learning, 73, 218, 219, 220, 225
insula, 14, 16, 32
interpersonal style, 74
introjection, 43, 44, 45, 233
introspection, 222, 223
Johari window, 109
Jones, Keith, 89
journaling, 202, 214, 222
Jung, Carl, 3
keeping short accounts, 103
Kegan & Lahey, 74, 176, 247, 253
Kelleher, Herb, 5, 241
King, Dr Martin Luther, 228

Kline, Nancy, 92, 248
leader as coach, 135, 139
leaning in, 219
level 5 leadership, 153
Life-Giving Workforce Design Model, 191, 195, 237, 254
limbic system, 12, 15, 18, 119
liminal experiences, 229
locus of control, 126, 231, 232, 233, 234, 236, 238
long-term goals, 217
lower anterior cingulate cortex, 15
loyalty to persons not present, 100
managing expectations, 101, 105
managing upwards, 123, 232, 249
Mandela, Nelson, 96
Marsden, George, 90
medication, 49
meditation, 16, 116, 202, 222, 229
memories, explicit, 13
memories, implicit, 13
mentoring, 2, 6, 73, 129, 132, 192, 220, 262
mind-body connection, 20
mini-self, 21, 22
mirror neurons, 17
misophonia, 130
monoculture, 83, 152
Morgan, Gareth, 2, 82, 108, 241
motivational needs, 61, 173
narcissism, 54, 205
needs, assertion, 62, 174
needs, attachment (see also attachment), 62
needs, physiological, 61
needs, sensual, 61
needs. aversion, 61
neurons, 12, 15, 16, 17, 18, 83, 101, 144, 179, 206, 220, 242
neuroplasticity, 11, 15, 84
NHS, 53, 79, 80, 82
Nicholson, Nigel, 169, 179, 253
numbing, 44
Oakwood Secondary Comprehensive School, 25
obsessive compulsive disorder, 52
outliers, 5, 151, 152, 237
oxytocin, 32
PACE, 113, 116, 117, 120, 121, 203, 237
panic disorder, 51
paranoia, 52
people, product and profit, 143, 193
perfectionism, 202

performance and development review, 131
performance management, 129, 250
personal development, 76, 95, 132, 202, 217, 218, 223, 238, 255
personal development, theories of, 73
personal growth groups, 221
personal mission statement, 215, 255
personality disorders, 49, 206
person-situation debate, 25
Peters, Steve, 12, 242
philosophy, 143, 184, 185, 227, 229
pituitary gland, 13
posterior cortex, 14
prefrontal cortex, 14, 15, 83, 168, 242
projection, 37, 39, 40, 41, 42, 43, 44, 95, 244
projection in groups, 41
projective identification, 40
PTSD, 16, 53, 55
redundancy, 57
Regret-Reason-Remedy, 71
relaxation practices, 202
reliability, 99, 100
religion, 76, 227, 228
resilience, personal, 125, 181, 199, 238
retroflection, 45
Rogers, Carl, 4, 92, 96, 107, 108, 109, 111, 113, 115, 248
role ambiguity, 57
rumination, 125
safe container, 119, 121, 167
scapegoat, 41, 82, 84
schizophrenia, 16
self-awareness, 70, 113, 115, 117, 167, 202
self-care, 201, 202
self-compassion, 5
self-disclosure, 110, 111
self-regulation, 96, 100, 115, 117, 202
self-sabotage, 26
self-transforming mind, 75, 76, 218
servant leadership, 152, 228
shadow work, 228
Siegel, Daniel, 17, 18, 20, 242, 243
Smith, Lynn, 89
social capital, 167, 169
socialized mind, 77, 95
sociopaths, 55, 95, 181, 205, 245, 255

sociopathy, 54, 55, 181, 182, 206, 207, 208, 209
soft thinking, 22
software apps, 64, 65, 247
spiritual path, 221, 238
STOP, 70, 116
stretch projects, 222
strong emotions, 119
supervision, 6, 137, 138, 220
swimming pool experiment, 97
synapse, 12
systemic thinking, 79
systems, characteristics of, 81
task versus process, 166
team development, 171
team maturity, 168
T-groups, 221
therapy, 6, 17, 27, 36, 49, 52, 57, 96, 131, 132, 208, 220, 221, 231
Thomas, Steve, 89
transactional analysis, 22, 67, 72, 103, 153, 251
transactions, crossed, 69
transactions, ulterior, 70
transcendence, 228
transference, 35, 37, 42, 244
transformational learning, 76, 77, 202, 218, 220, 225
trauma, 16, 21, 32, 91
travel, 222, 224
Traynor, Vincent, 41
trust, 30, 92, 99, 100, 101, 102, 103, 104, 105, 119, 144, 148, 149, 150, 155, 159, 160, 163, 167, 169, 175, 187, 188, 189, 221, 235, 248, 249
Tune, Ken, 1
unconditional positive regard, 107, 108, 111, 113, 130
unconscious mind, 20, 23, 25, 27, 231
unfinished business, 43, 57, 58, 59, 61, 103, 150, 157, 202, 203, 238, 245
vagus nerve, 20
vulnerability, 91, 95, 98, 99, 152, 237
Welch, Jack, 179, 211, 253, 255
Westgate, Ed, 5
Westgate, Tom, 5, 143
Whitehead, John, 11
window of tolerance, 5, 90, 93, 124, 125, 150, 151, 218, 229, 235
work intensification, 188
yoga, 116, 202, 222, 229, 262
ZOUD, 97, 98

TABLE OF FIGURES

Figure 1: The brain   13

Figure 2: A model of the mind (Bachkirova)   21

Figure 3: Abstract from the APMS 2014   50

Figure 4: A complementary transaction   68

Figure 5: A crossed transaction   69

Figure 6: Stages in adult development (Bachkirova)   74

Figure 7: Plateaus in adult mental development (Kegan & Lahey)   75

Figure 8: Subject and object in the three developmental stages   76

Figure 9: The individual in their system   81

Figure 10: The Johari window   109

Figure 11: Influencing styles   124

Figure 12: The line manager's role (Downey)   136

Figure 13: The circle of culture (after de Vries)   149

Figure 14: Hierarchical symbiosis (Hay)   154

Figure 15: The Kubler-Ross model of individual change   161

Figure 16: The task - process challenge (Bluckert)   166

Figure 17: Purpose, vision, strategy and behavioural norms   173

Figure 18: Typical output from an 'Immunity to Change' process   176

Figure 19: Flexible working trends - from the 2011 WERS   187

Figure 20: The Life-Giving Workforce Design Model   195

Figure 21: A model for personal resilience   200

Figure 22: A model for finding your vocation   213

Figure 23: Assembling a personal development plan   217

Figure 24: Routes to development   219

Figure 25: Dimensions of spirituality   228

Figure 26: A Compassionate leadership Meta Model   236

ABOUT THE AUTHOR

Chris Whitehead's career has spanned design engineering, academia, contracting, project investment, programme management, sustainability, and coaching. He has held senior management positions and directorships in several successful multinational businesses and three SMEs. At present, he runs a Sheffield-based coaching and mentoring company, Damflask Consulting.

Chris has a first-class honours degree from Trinity College Cambridge and an MBA from the University of Sheffield. He has a Postgraduate Certificate in coaching and mentoring from Sheffield Hallam University and is accredited by the European Mentoring and Coaching Council as a Senior Practitioner. He is a Fellow of the Institution of Civil Engineers.

He has been married for 37 years to Judi, his insightful and tireless personal coach, and they have three wonderful daughters. In his spare time, he can be found on a bike, in a yoga studio, at City of Sheffield Rowing Club or walking the hills of the Peak District National Park.

LinkedIn:	https://www.linkedin.com/in/chris-whitehead-b334ba20/
Website:	www.compassionate-leadership.co.uk
Blog:	https://medium.com/@chris_97488
Podcast:	The Compassionate Leadership Interview